PROCEEDS FROM THE AUTHOR'S PORTION OF THIS BOOK ARE BEING DONATED TO THE DANIEL J. MCGILLEN FOUNDATION FOR DOWN SYNDROME, INC.

ESTABLISHED BY MARY SANDERS SMITH IN HONOR OF HER GRANDCHILD BORN WITH DOWN SYNDROME, THE DANIEL J. MCGILLEN FOUNDATION IS COMMITTED TO IMPROVING THE WELFARE OF PEOPLE AFFLICTED WITH DOWN SYNDROME AND THEIR FAMILIES.

THE PURPOSE OF THIS FOUNDATION IS TO MAKE QUALIFYING DISTRIBUTIONS TO INDIVIDUALS AND ORGANIZATIONS WHOSE MISSION IS TO PROVIDE EDUCATIONAL AND FINANCIAL SUPPORT TO INDIVIDUALS WITH DOWN SYNDROME.

TO ORDER *JUNE* AND *LOVE TAKES*
CALL 1-866-390-9666

LOVE TAKES:
STORIES & SKETCHES

LOVE TAKES:
STORIES & SKETCHES

by

Mary Sanders Smith

LINTEL

24 Blake Lane
Middletown, NY 10940-7370

LOVE TAKES is a work of fiction. Characters, places, and events in these stories and sketches are fictitious and do not portray any actual persons, places, or events. Any similarity between the characters or events and actual persons or events is purely coincidental.

Grateful acknowledgment is made to the following publications and awards for stories appearing in this work: *Arizona Quarterly, University of Michigan Literary Review: RAJAH, Heritage, Belvidere Daily Republican, The Northern Reader, Detroit Women Writers Anthology 1999, Detroit Free Press: Short Fiction Award,* Pen Syndicated Fiction Award, Detroit Public Library Short Fiction Award.

Copyright 2002 by Mary Sanders Smith

ISBN 0-931642-35-3
Library of Congress Control Number: 2002102152

Cover Art by Cathy Ouchterloney
Cover Photograph by William Cofone
Book Design by Jake Spatz

LINTEL

24 Blake Lane
Middletown, NY 10940-7370
To order books:
866-390-9666

Dedication

To Lucretia Smith Paddock for listening

Love seeketh only Self to please
To bind another to its delight,
Joys in another's loss of ease,
And builds a Hell in Heaven's despite.

"The Little Vagabond" – William Blake

CONTENTS

CONFERENCE CALL 13
WHEN THE SAINTS... 27
LOVERS 36
SHADOWS 47
HOOKED 62
FOR BETTER OR WORSE 67
LAST CHRISTMAS 74
SILVER BELLS 79
DADDY'S GIRL 85
THE END OF PAINTING 94
HAPPY HOUR 108
SUBURBAN SANTAS 110
IN SIGHT 122
ERNIE'S GONE 126
SONG OF URSULA 129
FAREWELL 135
RUNNING 143
OCTOBER LOVE 155
UPSTAIRS 157
ATLAS CEDAR 165
HOUSE OF MIRRORS 170
LAST NIGHT'S HERO 175
STRIKE UP THE BAND 182
ON BEING ALONE 189

CONFERENCE CALL

"Line 2," she whispers handing Mr. Clifton the note.

Miss Price hurries out as usual, but before she closes the office door she overhears an exuberant "Darling, I'm so glad…"

She takes a deep breath, leans against the door and tells herself she has not overheard that.

Heart pounding, she heads for the women's lounge. "Cover the phone for me, Darlene?"

"Now where is Miss Priss off to in such a huff?" Darlene whispers to the girl seated at the desk behind her.

Miss Price has never succumbed to office chiding. She simply turns a deaf ear. Mere youngsters, she rationalizes.

Today, of all days, she finds herself trapped within the toilet stall when two typists enter, and one begins to describe a lurid date. Once the scenario begins, there is no way Miss Price can leave. A man had forced the young woman into a situation that was irreversible, and the saga that sweeps beneath the stall, inhaled full scale by Miss Price, is unbelievable. What do these people spend their time doing, she wonders. Her world has never involved sordid encounters. She, too, has had boyfriends, but none went to these extremes.

Thankfully, Miss Price emerges to an empty lounge, her

mind racing erratically. Desperately wanting to flush away her wild concerns, she washes her hands and looks up into the room-long mirror confronted by her thoughts. Loyalty to Mr. Clifton goes with the territory, she's always thought. A recent magazine article documenting "affairs" (she hates to even verbalize the word mentally) guaranteed they rarely last over fifteen months. She dries her hands.

Darlene stops her as she hurries back to her desk. "Mr. Clifton's asking for you, Miss Price."

"Oh, dear," she says hastening her tiny steps.

"What could be eatin' her intercom button?" Darlene hisses to her co-worker.

"Yes, Mr. Clifton, you want me?" cringing at her phrasing.

"Come in, Miss Price. Will you please make a reservation for two at the Club Sushi for one o'clock tomorrow?" Looking at his calendar he adds, "and please cancel my three o'clock conference call."

Miss Price smiles, as always.

Looking her square in the face he explains, "Mrs. Sherwood is an important client. Thank you, Miss Price."

This is how he always dismisses her, so very politely, never curtly. The way he says, "Thank you, Miss Price," always gives her an air of confidence, a sense of worth, and she tilts her head a jot higher as she leaves his office.

Why then does she feel embarrassed asking the maitre d' to reserve a table for two for tomorrow? Never mind, she tells herself. She's made luncheon reservations many times before and never questioned it. How does she know what went on before or even now for that matter. Mr. Clifton is such a reliable family man. She can't help wondering if Mrs. Clifton knows Mr. Clifton's having lunch with a very important client whom he calls "Darling."

Usually, five o'clock is here before she knows it. Today her eyes check the clock at four, four-fifteen, then four-thirty when suddenly Mr. Clifton emerges to go over tomorrow's schedule. He leans very close, his silver hair faintly brushing hers. She can smell him, quite a pleasant odor, really. She flushes. Relieved to have him looking over her shoulder, no eye contact, she feels a tinge of comfort that soothes her.

"You may leave early tomorrow, Miss Price." Kind as he is, Mr. Clifton has never said that except when his father-in-law died unexpectedly.

Miss Price avoids Darlene on her way out, positioning herself on the far side of a group leaving the office. She escapes Darlene's eye unnoticed.

On the way home in the bus Miss Price sits perplexed. What is sex, she wonders — she's always wondered. Does it have anything to do with love? Once in a while she feels stirring sensations when Mr. Clifton leans near her or the vegetable man at the market lays his hand on her arm and stands too close, but that's not love. Occasionally, she ponders why she never married, but not marrying seems quite normal to her now, not at all strange. She accepts that certain uncontrollable events intervened during the time when she'd had a boyfriend. External happenings such as the war had simply separated her from some beau for too long a time to consider marriage.

Of all her boyfriends, she liked Harold the best. He'd been about her size — they were much the same, went to some dances together in high school. Her parents liked him, as well. Strange that now she can't really remember what had separated them. He must have moved away, perhaps during the summer. Surely, she'd have remembered if it had been during the school year.

The bus jogs her back and forth as it starts and stops, intermittently depositing passengers. Miss Price hardly notices. She almost forgets to get off at her bus stop, but at the last minute she recognizes her corner, the familiar red climbing roses long ago having become one with the white picket fence. Usually this seasonal profusion delights her. Today she barely sees it as she steps off the bus. Ordinarily, she savors the colorful display, stopping to acknowledge the loveliest blooms, giving each winner her approval. She never regrets not picking one. Although often tempted, she knows this variety could never survive once removed from its life source. The plants' repetitive continuity comforts her. They bloom all summer long. She's grown to love the red and white scene outlining the black-shuttered bungalow at her bus stop.

Sometimes, while waiting for the bus, she tries to sort out what goes on inside the house. Rarely does she see anyone outside. In the winter when it gets dark early, yellow-lit shadows behind veiled windows offer the best view. She can't help imagining a scenario or two: dinner delayed while feeding the baby, anticipating a late husband's arrival, cuddling a child that has coughed all night long with croup. Fall croup demands so much attention.

When it's dark, she slows her pace along the rose-defined fence, but always turns away a little resentful at the brevity of her glimpses, hoping for one more prolonged insight. After all, it's only a small portion of their lives she is stealing, nothing they would ever miss. They could afford her a bit more exposure before drawing the shade. Curtained off, it's hard to dream on.

Right now it pains her to think of families in their cozy worlds, all mixed up with Mr. Clifton's new important client. It's too complicated to sort out.

A smell of pot roast fills the hall as she enters their first floor flat. During the week Gretchen comes in to cook for Miss Price and her mother.

Next morning, Priscilla Price rises to her alarm feeling as though night has been going on forever. Walking to the bus is like sleep walking. Every morning she sits in the same seat on the bus. It's always waiting for her. She doesn't know any of the bus riders' names. They exchange nods and sometimes greetings but would never encroach on another's seat.

Her head suddenly jerks, and she realizes she must have fallen asleep momentarily. Embarrassed, she glances about furtively to see if any of the other regulars noticed her nodding off. Everyone's reading their newspapers or looking out the window. Everything below the headlines is a blur. Three topics dominate today's news: Russia, murder, and sex. The thought of exploring any one of these depresses her.

Riding up the elevator in a fog, she almost misses the blue rug on the 23rd floor. All the floors look alike, except for their varying colors. Blue is the clue to her floor. But they aren't even true colors according to Miss Price's rainbow. Primary colors have apparently disappeared from the spectrum. Actually she works on Muted Teal, she was told, after the most recent office refurbishing.

"Good morning, Darlene," Miss Price mumbles.

"Good morning," Darlene echoes.

Once Miss Price turns the corridor corner, Darlene whirls to her counterpart. "Something's wrong with Miss Cool, Phyllis."

"I thought she was Miss Priss — "

"Depends upon which direction she's headed."

Miss Price enters her sparse office. She keeps meaning

to hang that picture of an English countryside her mother gave her last Christmas. "Your office lacks luster, Priscilla," her mother had said.

Mr. Clifton bounds in with his usual, "Good day, Miss Price. Don't you look perky today!"

Numbed from lack of sleep, she smiles weakly at him. She's almost forgotten yesterday's episode when her phone rings, but a familiar voice spins her back. She'd know that voice anywhere now.

Icily, she responds, "I'll see if Mr. Clifton is in, Mrs. Sherwood." She couldn't imagine *throwing herself* on a man like that.

"Clifton here?" an elderly partner asks, heading straight for Mr. Clifton's door.

"He's on the phone."

"Oh, he always sees me," and walks briskly into Mr. Clifton's office.

Through the half-opened door she can see Mr. Clifton's expression change from ecstasy to marked disapproval.

Later Mrs. Sherwood calls again. Miss Price tries to soften her tone. A moment later, however, Mrs. Clifton is on the phone to speak to her husband, and Miss Price wonders if she is up to all this. Nervously, she takes in the message.

"Tell her I'm on a conference call. I'll call her back."

Conference call? She asks herself. This is no three-way conversation.

Poor thing, Miss Price thinks, racing back to relay the message.

At 12:30 Mr. Clifton emerges from his office announcing his departure for the Club Sushi. Miss Price notices his new brown suit and paisley tie. Quite nice, she thinks, especially with his white hair. Ordinarily she might say, "Have a nice lunch," but somehow she can't bring herself to say it today.

"Why don't you go for lunch now, too, Miss Price? Take some extra time."

Before she can answer, Mrs. Clifton appears in the doorway.

"Oh, Rob, I'm so glad I caught you. You didn't call me back, so I thought I'd surprise you. We can have lunch — a date," she laughs, flipping her hair flirtatiously, "you know, at some romantic spot."

Miss Price looks from one to other. Is Mrs. Clifton serious?

Mr. Clifton never skips a beat. "Why, Mary, what a nice surprise, but I have a business lunch, dear. I thought I mentioned it this morning." He hesitates. "I have an idea, Mary dear, why don't you and Miss Price go somewhere and have a nice quiet lunch together? You keep mentioning you want to do that. Pick a nice restaurant, Miss Price — somewhere you've always wanted to go," he says generously. "How about that new place 'Chez Moi'? It's close by."

"Oh, no, I couldn't..." Miss Price begins.

"Of course, you can, Miss Price," Mrs. Clifton interjects. "You go on now, Rob. We'll get on fine. That explains your being all dressed up."

"See you tonight, love," and kisses his wife good-bye.

Miss Price does a double-take as Mr. Clifton winks at her on his way out.

Utterly confused by the whole scene, Miss Price gathers her coat, thinking, at least she knows where *not* to take Mrs. Clifton.

Mary Clifton spends the entire lunch hour praising Miss Price. "How lucky Rob is to have you, Miss Price. What would we do without you, Miss Price? What a gem you are, Miss Price. How did we ever get along without you, Miss Price? Rob has such trust in you, Miss Price."

Miss Price, Miss Price, Miss Price rings on and on clanging in her head like dozens of church belfries chiming twelve-noon all at once, compounding her guilt with each crescendo. She feels faint, overburdened by the cacophonous messages, realizing that she actually feels responsible for Mr. Clifton's infidelity. How could this be? How had she become part of this ugly conspiracy? Was it when he winked at her? Yes, that was it. He'd brought her in on his little tryst with a simple wink of his eye. How could she possibly resent an innocent wink of the eye. At least she'd not responded, or had she? Perhaps she'd returned an inadvertent knowing smile. She must be more careful.

Once back at the office, stepping from the elevator, Miss Price feels absolutely exhausted.

"Something's definitely slowed her up," Darlene points out to Phyllis. "Like she got her dress caught in the revolving door and spent the lunch hour tryin' to pull it loose. She looks like hell."

Slumping into her desk chair, Miss Price is glad to have plenty of typing to keep her busy this afternoon. She won't leave early after all, as if she could be bribed. If only Mrs. Clifton hadn't mentioned trusting her. She must think of other matters. She thinks of taking early retirement.

Priscilla Price has been with Mr. Robert Clifton for over ten years and Mr. Preston Hardwick twenty years before that. She's outlasted most secretaries in the office. It was a good position for her after Mr. Hardwick died. Poor Mr. Hardwick, he hadn't deserved such a fate, but she can't atone for that. She'd done her job. Doing her job has always given her so much satisfaction.

When Miss Price takes a break and heads for the Ladies', as Darlene delicately puts it, Darlene checks her watch. "Right on schedule, see that, Phyllis? She's not so off track as I'd thought. Guess I'll split for a drag."

Miss Price is safely in a toilet stall when she overhears Darlene say, "Well, what's new in the high-rise syndrome world, Meg?" She pictures Darlene leaning against the wash basin and offering Meg a cigarette.

"Hmm, let's see. Did you hear Sue is cheating on her hours billed?"

"That's *news*?"

"I figger'd you'd know that one. Hey, I've been raggin' on everybody today — sorry. So, what's with Miss Priss? I hear she's all a-twit..."

"Shh... back off," Darlene whispers.

Quickly Miss Price flushes the toilet, almost forgets to powder herself, and then emerges as though she's not heard a word. What could they know, anyway, she thinks. She'll not breathe a word to a soul. Smiling a little too pleasantly she sidles around to an open basin.

Darlene moves to give her room — "Here, Miss Price" — changing the conversation to her cancelled Club Med weekend cruise next month. "My insignificant other can't go," she moans, "my roommate can't afford it, and, I can't swing a single."

Before the lounge door closes behind Miss Price, she hears Darlene sigh, "Whew! I hope she didn't hear you."

"So what's with all the pity?"

"I don't know, I feel kinda sorry for her lately. She looks kinda tired, and I don't know — sickly."

"Oh, yeah, when did you get off so generous — maybe you're sickly," Meg laughs. "Now, give me the scoop on Miss Priss."

"Honestly, I don't know what's up. I just know somethin' screwy's goin' on, though — don't worry, I'll find out."

Meg laughs, "We count on you, Darlene."

#

On Friday, Mr. Clifton greets Miss Price jauntily, "Good day, Miss Price. Don't you look nice today!"

Miss Price tries to put the past few days out of her mind. If Mrs. Sherwood just wouldn't call. Miss Price has no idea if Mr. Clifton calls her.

Later that afternoon Darlene pops into her room, "Heads up, Miss Price. Whoops — didn't mean to scare ya. How 'bout chaperoning the crew over at 'Capers' Hall of Infamy after work?"

"Oh, my, I don't think so — it's very kind of you, though. We always have an early dinner on Fridays. I take Momma to Bingo. She looks forward to it, but thank you anyway."

"We'll catch ya some other night. Take care now."

Puzzled by Darlene's peace offering, Miss Price wonders what prompted it. Maybe she *should* join them sometime. It does get tiresome ignoring their snide remarks.

Hurrying off the bus, Miss Price buttons her coat against an early autumn chill. She stops to examine the roses that have opened that day. The blooms are especially large. Somewhat sadly, she realizes this is the final blooming for the clinging vine and thinks it odd that these last blooms should be the most lovely when by all rights the plant should have spent itself on earlier blossoms. She doesn't quite understand the logic, the justification of one last spurt. Is it the eternal yearning for rebirth? Perhaps it's simply the urge to shine just one more time, to know again that youth in love — even though the action may damage or even kill the roots, that very base from which daily sustenance comes. It's as though she were looking at Mr. Clifton, at some latent bud mysteriously swelling to bloom exuberantly one last time. She scowls to imagine it's triggered by that shameless woman.

She resists the urge to clip all the mounting protuberances before they can burst forth to victimize the bush and act as though it were the beginning when, in fact, it is the end. It would make sense to prune them now — she's known wise gardeners to recommend it.

#

Mr. Clifton enters the office mid-morning on Monday. Miss Price has been restless, thinking it quite strange for Mr. Clifton to be so late.

"Any calls?"

"Your conference call is scheduled in a few minutes."

"By the way, Miss Price. Will you please pick up a package at Neiman's for me this noon? Don't worry if you're late getting back from lunch." He smiles, "A little something for Mrs. Clifton."

How nice, thinks Miss Price. She hopes they had a nice weekend.

The sales person insists on opening the merchandise for Miss Price's inspection. "Oh, dear, no," she protests. "I'm just picking this up for my employer."

"But the initialing must be approved. It's our policy or I cannot release the item."

"Very well, then," and Miss Price proceeds to examine the back of a beautiful diamond brooch engraved with the message, LOVE, RJC encircled within a heart. Satisfied, Miss Price asks for the package to be wrapped.

Toward the end of the day, Mr. Clifton tells Miss Price that Mrs. Sherwood will be coming into the office later this week, on Thursday, to be exact, around noon, and he will accompany her to lunch. Miss Price is to cancel any conflicting engagements. Shocked at this bit of news, she's determined not to let herself dwell on the prospect of meeting this woman. Perhaps she could be ill and stay home that day. She cannot imagine meeting this woman face to face. No doubt she dyes her hair and wears a lot of makeup. Miss Price pictures her sitting at a vanity dabbing into this jar and that, covering her skin with rejuvenating creams and lotions, never allowing clean soap and water to touch her face. Miss Price always considered dyed hair and too much makeup *cheap.*

"I might be a little late coming back from my meeting today, Miss Price," Mr. Clifton announces Thursday morning. "Please make Mrs. Sherwood comfortable in my office. You know what to do, bring her some coffee, keep her company."

Miss Price chokes on her coffee, unable to answer.

"Oh, oh," Darlene says to Phyllis as Miss Price speeds past to the ladies' lounge. "She's upset again — I can tell — her waddle changes — must make her bladder act up — sure wonder what's goin' on in Clifton's office."

Mid-morning Darlene checks in on Miss Price. "Just thought I'd ask if you'd come with us this Friday night. You could bring Momma," she laughs. "Seriously, I thought maybe you could make some other plans for Momma if you knew ahead. Don'tcha have a cousin or someone like that to take her?"

Darlene's laugh relaxes Miss Price. "You know, I think I might just do that, Darlene. Thanks for thinking of me."

"That's Okay. We'll grab a pizza there. You like pizza?"

Miss Price nods.

Right now she's too preoccupied worrying about Mrs. Sherwood's arrival to question Darlene's friendliness. It sounded sincere, but she's not sure about anything anymore.

Darlene buzzes Miss Price, announcing Mr. Clifton's client is waiting in the reception room.

Leading Mrs. Sherwood down the hall, Miss Price avoids looking at her. She ushers her into Mr. Clifton's office, offering to take her coat and bring some coffee. Does Mrs. Sherwood know Mr. Clifton will be a few minutes late? Yes? Oh, good. Sugar and cream or black? Miss Price reacts like a robot. Upon returning, she finally takes a good look at Mrs. Sherwood. Her eyes cannot get past Mrs. Sherwood's suit lapel. Frozen, Miss Price stares. She's wearing Mrs. Clifton's brooch! How could she!

"The ph-phone," Miss Price stammers, "excuse me," and bolts from the room.

It isn't until Mr. Clifton ushers Mrs. Sherwood, arm in hand, out of the office, that she realizes what an attractive woman Mrs. Sherwood is. She's never seen one of *those* women before. Miss Price doesn't like her one whit more now that she's laid eyes on her either.

By Friday, Miss Price is ready for the weekend. She's even looking forward to going out with Darlene's office group.

On her way to the women's lounge mid-morning, Miss Price notices Darlene is away from her desk. She smiles at Phyllis in passing, stooping to pick up a stray paper clip on the floor and drops it into the container on Darlene's desk.

Once ensconced in her favorite toilet stall, however, she feels the weight of the usually friendly walls looming inward, pressing in on her. She feels trapped, no longer safe. Anxious to escape, she emerges into the open lounge. The endless row of toilet stalls confronts her stretching to infinity, reflected one after another in the mirrors, reminding her of small metal cages where no one can see in or out, where only sounds penetrate. Distressed, she hurries to leave. In the quiet of the softly lit hall, Miss Price catches her breath and smooths her hair before heading back to her office.

Right after lunch, Mrs. Sherwood calls Mr. Clifton, and Miss Price knows not to disturb *that* conference call. She doesn't even take messages in anymore, just saves them until they finish talking. However, when Mrs. Clifton calls sounding rather urgent, she's unsure of what to do next.

Deferring to his wife, Miss Price chooses to interrupt Mr. Clifton with the message and puts Mrs. Clifton on hold. As though in slow motion, she walks toward the inner office door. But then just as she touches the doorknob, she changes her mind, whirls about and returns to her desk. Eyeing the line where Mrs. Clifton waits to speak with her husband, Miss Price smooths her hair and with her free hand she plugs Mrs. Clifton in on the conference call.

WHEN THE SAINTS...

Teresa crossed her arms on the round oak table and lowered her head to rest on the back of her hands. The hall clock struck nine. Tom would be home from work soon. She was unbearably tired and longed to sleep, escape, if only for a few minutes.

She woke with a start as Tom kissed her forehead. "How's the Saint?" he asked affectionately. "Big day?"

"Please."

It was bad enough when her son Stanton called her "The Saint," but it was even worse to hear Tom say it, affectionately or not. The name had become a command, however difficult.

"I'm not a saint, Tom." Teresa roused herself, frowning. "I don't even have your supper ready."

"Don't fuss," Tom said, smoothing stray damp hair from her forehead. "You've already eaten. I'll rustle up something after I've changed — be down in a minute."

Like a robot she moved through her once comforting kitchen, now seemingly strange, off-limits to her. Her mind raced defensively. It's like a put-down, being called "The Saint," playing off my inadequacies, making me feel guilty for *not* being a Saint.

She set Tom's place and made him a salad. It was hard to believe that only yesterday her life had been normal. Somehow she'd managed to get through today. She heard the children upstairs, too tired to respond to their quarreling.

"Shut up, you creep. Get out of my room. Mother!" Mary Ann yelled.

"Is that so!" Stanton teased. Teresa could imagine his feet planted just outside the limits of a line which defined Mary Ann's private territory. He would thrust his lanky body tauntingly forward into his older sister's sanctuary. "So, you're calling in the Saint."

"Don't call her that! Oh!" Mary Ann exploded. "You get away with murder, just by calling her *The Saint.*"

Teresa winced. What will they think of me now, she wondered, the children, Tom. How can I tell them? She cringed inwardly with the shame of remembering what she had done today. In truth, she was scared to death, and seemed as far away as one could get from being a Saint.

Was it only this morning she'd pulled up to the Valet Parking at Ford Hospital? On the way to the twelfth floor for her physical exam she read the sign in the elevator that warned against muggers, how one should be aware of what might seem like an inadvertent side-swipe or rear-ender. She found this hard to believe when day after day in her safe suburban community, she left her house open and her car unlocked.

Once back in her car Teresa buckled her seat belt and turned onto the street, relieved to find no traffic. It had snowed a little while she was seeing the doctor, so she drove slowly at first.

All of a sudden the car lurched, and she was slammed

forward, then backwards against the seat. Angry at being hit, she was about to put the car in park and get out when she looked in the rear view mirror. Two big men emerged from the car behind and walked toward her. The elevator sign — "CAUTION: STAY IN YOUR CAR — PROCEED TO NEAREST POLICE." Slamming the accelerator to the floor, she swerved around the corner, her car almost out of control as she jerked at the steering wheel. She must escape. Aimed for the ramp leading to the freeway, the car lurched dangerously to the right.

"If I can just make it to the freeway." Suddenly, a woman loomed directly in front of the hood.

She must have closed her eyes because a few seconds later speeding down the freeway she realized what she'd done. She'd hit a woman and even worse had driven off, left the scene of an accident. Her temple throbbed.

Did I really hit her? Maybe not. She wasn't sure. It had all happened so fast. Oh, God, she thought, maybe I killed her. She couldn't remember the car hitting anything. Maybe she'd missed her, maybe the woman had jumped out of the way. Teresa tried to remember.

How many times had she told the kids not to leave the scene of an accident. What if those men were only coming to check for damage. Maybe they hadn't been muggers. Well, she had a legitimate excuse for leaving. Even if the men had taken down her license plate number, she could always tell the police about the notice in the elevator. But hit and run?

"Crime." It had such a dreadful ring to it. "Does that make me a criminal?" She'd always attached that word to people she'd read about in the newspaper, posters on the wall of the post office, never herself.

Pulling into her garage, she turned off the motor and sat

immobilized. Heat waves trembled from the car hood. For the moment she felt safe here at home until she began to wonder if she'd been followed. Unsure of what to do next, she forced herself to get out and look for damage. Her legs felt weak. There was only a small dent in the rear bumper. She hurried around to the front to see if she could find a mark from hitting someone. There was none. She sighed with relief. Surely there would be some evidence if she'd hit the woman.

She walked into the house half expecting to hear the phone ringing, suspecting the worst, like the police saying she was wanted for murder. But the phone hung silently in its cradle. Teresa stared at it. She must not get hysterical. She would call the emergency room and find out whether a woman had been hit by a car in front of the hospital. She had to know that much.

A woman's voice answered, "Emergency, Ford Hospital."

Teresa hesitated, "Uh — uh, did a woman…?" She stuttered, "I'm calling for a friend, was a woman admitted who was hit by a car early this afternoon?"

"Who's calling, please? Hello, hello — "

Teresa hung up the phone. She would have to think of something else. She looked about for something to keep her busy. She decided to scrub the floor before the kids came home from school but half-way through knew she had to call again. This time she would make up a name.

A different voice answered. "This is Mona Brown," Teresa said, "I'm inquiring about the condition of the woman who was hit earlier, around noon, out in front of the hospital."

"Are you a relative?"

"No," said Teresa.

"The patient's name?"
"Uh, I don't know," Teresa said. "I just saw it happen."
"Please hold."
Another voice came on the phone. "I'm sorry, we can't give out that information. Who IS THIS calling please?"
Teresa hung up, convinced now that the woman had been admitted, and that they suspected her. She jumped as the back door slammed. The kids were home from early dismissal. She could not risk calling again. Every hour that passed removed her further from detection. Under the protective cloak of her kitchen she felt safe, far removed from the scene. Still a dreadful morbid feeling clung to her. She was already thinking like a criminal.
"Hi, Mom!" Stanton said, and a wave of guilt shivered through her. It'd been a pretense all along, being called a Saint, and now her real self had come out. The criminal, the unsaintly side of her had finally emerged, that part of her that had always been there locked within, waiting to expose itself.
Wandering aimlessly about the house, she picked something up here and put it down there, searching for what to do next. She'd give anything for a moment's peace, forget herself in routine. Boredom would seem glorious.
After serving Tom his late dinner, she managed to clean up the kitchen. Her sanctuary was remote and alien. Utterly alone, removed from her family, it was as though she were a numbed spectator, an observer watching all this happen to someone else. She climbed the stairs to bed.
Sleep came fast at first but was quickly followed by a tossing restlessness. She was not sure whether she was dreaming or awake. She was somewhere between yesterday and today and then suddenly swallowed by a weird

dream.

Stanton followed Tom into the kitchen and perched himself on the counter top in that good-natured manner of his, kicking his heels, one at a time, against the cupboard door.

"I can't take much noise this time of night," Teresa teased gently.

Tom sat eating a salad.

"That reminds me," he said, lifting his fork toward Stanton. "I thought of you today at lunch."

"Oh yeah?"

"Well, I saw the name of this new cafe across the street, and it said 'STANTON'S' — and I thought how we'd have to go there, all of us together, but then on second glance, there was a little period after the first T, so it really said 'ST. ANTON'S.' Then, I had to laugh because now you're a Saint, just like you call Mom, AND you're the son of a Saint."

"Whatever," Stanton said.

"Serves you right, Stanton, nick-naming everyone," Teresa laughed, giving Stan a hug. She held him at arm's length. "Tell me, St. Anton, did you finish your homework yet?"

Stanton shrugged, trying his best not to smile and slipped down from the counter.

Her dream disappeared like a deflated New Year's Eve blow toy, and she lay in bed fully awake. So as not to wake Tom, she rose slowly and walked to the window.

How had Stanton anointed her so long ago? "Don't tease Mom," he'd said to his sister. "Why, that woman's a Saint!"

At first it had sounded funny though outrageous was more like it. Now she realized it wasn't funny at all. She longed to wriggle out of it like an overripe caterpillar.

Outside, a moon pocked with dark clouds moved across the sky. Kaleidoscopic patterns wrecked any sense of order, suffocating her. Was there no limit? Could guilt become so profound that one day it would be so unbearable it would wear itself out? She turned from the window, afraid she might have turned her back on peace of mind forever.

She flicked on the light over the bathroom mirror wincing at her pale reflection. She looked tired, exhausted from her lie. It saddened her to think she could talk like this to no one except the mirror. Were human beings the only creatures condemned to consequences, to carry the burdens of responsibility plus the guilt? What about all the animals that hid in their crevices? Didn't jaguars make mistakes?

She knew what she *should* do. She should call the police.

Tomorrow was Saturday. She would wait to call until Tom went to the office. Mary Ann would be baby-sitting and Stanton at swimming practice.

She must have fallen asleep after all because Tom was dressed and gone when she woke. She looked at the bedside clock. It was after nine. Both children would be gone by now. She put on her robe, walked downstairs to the kitchen and went right to the phone. At last she got through to the police station near the hospital.

"This is Teresa Ross," she began. "I'm calling to confess, to turn myself in." Tears came, and for a moment she could not continue.

"Yes ma'am," the policeman said.

"I think I hit a woman in front of Ford Hospital, about noon yesterday on my way home, and I left the scene of the accident. Tell me, did I kill her?" Teresa asked.

"Hold on a minute, I'll look up the record."

Teresa held her breath while the policeman checked the records.

"Ma'am?" he returned to the phone. "I can't find any report of a hit-and-run in that area yesterday, all day long, in fact."

"You must be mistaken. Have you checked thoroughly?"

"Thoroughly, ma'am. But give me your name and phone number again."

Teresa tried to speak. In the background she could hear phones ringing. "Teresa Ross," she finally said, "886-4615."

"We have an emergency here, ma'am. I have to hang up now."

With a dazed look Teresa stared at the dead phone in her hand. "He probably thought I was just another kook."

No flood of relief followed with the discovery that she had committed no crime. Instead a nagging remorse remained. She should have called the police immediately.

Stanton stood in the kitchen doorway staring at her. She looked up at him, speechless.

"What happened? What did you do?" he blurted out. "Kill someone? Was that the police? Will you go to prison?" He turned away and stared out the window. "Well?"

His questions tore into her, and her only response was a torrential release of tears. At length she was able to say between sobs, "I guess I didn't hit the woman, after all." She hesitated, then continued, "But I didn't know that until just now. I did a terrible thing, Stanton. I ran away, thinking I had hit her." She wanted him to hug her like she'd hugged him a thousand times. She hid her face in her hands.

Stanton looked down at his sneakers awkwardly shifting his weight from one foot to the other.

"Well, I'd better get to practice."

"Yes, I suppose you'd better."

Teresa cringed as the back door slammed harder than usual behind Stanton, running into Mary Ann as he left.

"So where's my tennis racket, Stanton? I need it."

"How should I know?" he snapped, jumping on his bike.

Teresa watched him from where he'd left her. He slowed as he passed the window, and their eyes met.

"Hey, Mary Ann," a broad smile on his face, "go ask the Saint!"

LOVERS

    She was glad now that she had paid the extra fare to fly first class. The flight attendants were nicer. The seats were wider, and no one sat next to her. She wanted to be alone, to role-play in the closets of her mind, no idle chatter from some well-meaning traveler.

    "It was *my* decision," she would say. She simply would tell him outright. "I'm leaving your father. We're separating," just like Bill had told her his decision six years before when he'd called home that day.

    "Mother," Bill had said, "remember when I talked to you about Clare?"

    Susan tried to remember.

    Bill was silent at the other end of the line.

    "Yes?" Susan hesitated, still trying to remember who Clare was.

    "Well," Bill announced, "Clare and I are living together."

    It was Susan's turn to be silent.

    "Mother, are you there?"

    "I don't know what to say, Bill — I don't know what to say. I don't even know how I feel about this. I think I have to hang up and think a while. I'll call you back."

Susan's mind went blank after hanging up the phone. She sat in the kitchen chair, elbows resting on the cool formica counter. She wanted to feel something, anger, embarrassment, cheated, anything! She looked about the kitchen — everything was the same. The stove light was on. The clock had not stopped ticking. The dishwasher was running. Even the faucet still dripped.

She was not sure how long she sat there when she began to worry about telling Bill's father that night. Should she just blurt it out — "Bill's living with someone!" — the minute he walked in the door? And would Carl demand, "With whom?" in his almost angry voice that always made Susan feel guilty, as though she'd missed the boat somewhere along the line raising their son.

She thought of their friends who gossiped about so-and-so's *living* with someone. Playing house was what Susan had called it, can't make a decision, no commitment, copping out. Was she going to feel differently now that *her* son was doing it?

Just then the phone rang again. Susan lifted the receiver.

"Actually, Mother, Clare and I are married," Bill blurted out. "We were married two weeks ago. We had a regular wedding and all," as if that made it all right.

"Why didn't you tell us?" Susan said, trying to stay calm, controlling her mounting hurt.

"Because I knew you'd say 'no.'"

It was as simple as that, no complicated explanations, no lies, no threats, no fights. He was right, Susan thought. We would have said no. He took that responsibility away from us.

His role had changed that very minute. He was still her

son, yet not her son. Even the word sounded different as she repeated it to herself, first silently, then aloud, "son — son." It took on a new dimension, but she was not sure what. A flood of relief swept through her, like a revelation — she was no longer responsible for him.

She'd responded like a good mother — hadn't she? — accepting what he'd done and loving him more for it. Now, would he accept what she had done — would *mother* take on a new meaning now that there was no father attached?

Susan glanced up as yellow streaks from the fasten-seat-belt sign danced before her eyes. She turned away. Muscles tightened in her neck as tension mounted, and she stiffened into an upright position, grabbing the armrests. Aware of an increased roar from the plane's engine, she listened for a change in the motor's sound. She'd never felt comfortable flying, never quite accepted the fact that anything heavier than air could stay aloft, but a steady rhythm droned on. She pushed the button on her armrest and leaned back to relax.

Did Bill know all along she would accept whatever he did — did he trust that she would respect his decision? Did he know way back then about finding his own identity apart from her — and now, would he accept her new identity apart from his father?

Perhaps she should have told him about her decision to leave Carl when she called to say she was coming to Dallas.

Bill and Clare would meet her at the airport. She would have three hours with them before continuing on to Arizona. They would have dinner together at the airport. Hardly enough time, Susan thought. *Three years* wouldn't be long enough.

Now she was unsure how she should tell them. Maybe she should wait, call them from Arizona, but something told her to be honest and open. Pretending was shallow and unfair. But hadn't she been pretending all along, all these years pretending the inadequacies didn't matter?

No one's perfect, she told herself. She shouldn't have expected miracles.

She looked out the window at green-patched territories etched with tan seam binding. It was growing dark. Dim light from the cabin reflected the contents on her tray table in the small window. Superimposed on the patchwork land below were a small empty bottle of vodka, a yellow can of tonic and empty peanut wrappers. Constant and solid on the table in front of her, they moved when seen in the window, first covering a lake, then a small cluster of buildings with shining pinpoint lights. Or was the land below in motion?

How different the vodka and tonic looked in reflection. On the tray they were but a small contribution within the aircraft, but in the window they loomed large, taking on a new form, covering perhaps a whole county. Solid and tangible on the tray, in the window they became transparent and she could see right through them. Yet, what she saw on the faraway ground was only what the reflected images would allow her to see. At once distant and close, she could create the transparency by straining to look beyond. Changing contrasts were clouding her absolutes. Could nothing remain the same?

Now it was becoming dark, and the ground below was fading from view, leaving the mirrored vodka and tonic alone in the window, looking almost as solid as they did on the tray table. At length, she could see nothing below and closed her eyes to the dizzying effect of nothing fitting together. She pulled down the shade and turned away from the window.

"Would you care for another cocktail?" The flight attendant leaned over to collect the empty bottle, can and wrappers.

"No, thank you," she said and watched as piece by piece her entertainment disappeared into the trash bag.

The flight attendant turned to a couple across the aisle. "May I serve you some more wine?"

"Why not?" the man answered, reddening with a teen-aged embarrassment as he turned to his wife for approval.

To Susan, they looked very young, seemingly having a good time, not saying much. The young woman flipped through pages of *Vogue* magazine, then closed it to stare out the window into the dark. The flight attendant returned with their wine. The couple spoke to each other off and on, occasionally exchanging tiny smiles as they sipped their wine.

The flight attendant moved along the aisle from one passenger to the next. Another young couple across the aisle sat in the front row. Susan quickly decided they were not married to each other. She overheard snatches of excited conversation as they told each other about themselves. It amazed her how airplane trips could evoke intimate conversations between strangers as if they had only the length of a flight to spew out a lifetime, tell all before landing. How practiced the woman was in her timing, waiting until the man took a breath before jumping in to speak. How easily these strangers spoke with each other, how freely they exchanged their lives.

Perhaps she should have sat next to the handsome dark-haired man poring over what looked like legal briefs or maybe the pleasant looking grey-haired lady sitting alone two seats back.

Were people always looking for something from each other — be it family, friend or stranger? Exactly what did she expect from Bill? Did she want to be led by the hand through and around life's rubble: Be careful, Mother, don't catch your heel. Watch out for that hole. Don't rip those nylons. Is that what she wanted? But was she wrong to expect him to see her as something other than his mother, that special person who was at once everything and at the same time nothing? She was afraid Bill would not want to know *this* woman en route to see him, en route to disrupt his absolutes.

Snatches of conversation from the couple behind her annoyingly invaded her thoughts. She'd seen the couple in the gate area, standing too close to each other, he much older than she. Must be a second marriage, Susan thought, as words poured around and over her seat. They must be having another drink.

"Of course, you'll like Paris, darling," the male voice said. "You can buy the right clothes over there — don't fuss. Yes, a lot of people speak English. Of course, they know me at the Ritz."

Muffled giggles emerged. Susan pictured the woman's head on his shoulder, his face nuzzling her hair.

What if Bill asks why, Susan began to worry. He thinks everything is great, all is well. And why shouldn't he? After all, we were one big loving family at Christmas — holding hands at the table while his father said grace, thanking God for our being together, thanking God for each other. Where did it go wrong — stop ringing true?

Bill wants so much for everything to be all right, she thought. Does she have to tell him everything? Does he want to know about the loneliness, the put-downs, the petty inane arguments that resolved nothing and ended in uncontrollable frustration? Should she say there's no more love or respect — "I wish I could love your father, but I can't"?

She wished she could say there had been infidelity, if only it was that simple. All the reasons seemed clear one moment, nebulous the next.

Should she tell Bill that she would probably still be there, back with his father, but for a small, silly incident? It was so unimportant it embarrassed her to think it had triggered her leaving. Just last Saturday morning — hard to believe it was this last week, when the whole matter already seemed a thing of the past.

Returning from his round of morning errands, Carl had asked her, "Did anyone call for me?"

"I don't know," she said. "I just walked in."

Flashing an angry look, he said, "I was expecting a call. I thought you knew that."

"You didn't say anything to me."

"I didn't know you were leaving," he snarled.

Nothing any longer made sense. What was this madness they were living? The realization came to her plainly, not in anger, this time. She simply made a decision, "Yes, I am leaving." He did not stop her.

It hurt to think back on that moment, but she knew plain as day, it had been a long time in the making. The final confrontation had been so small but stood for so many of the *smalls* that came before.

Susan jumped when the intercom blared, "We will be landing soon. Please bring your seat forward." She tried to smile as the flight attendant passed by for one last check.

Raising her window shade, she looked down at the metropolitan area. Red beacons burned through a mass of brilliant white lights outlining downtown Dallas. She yawned to unplug her ears. The night was cloudless. Brilliant stars proclaimed their antiquity. Bright lights punctuated the runway. Nothing was left to the imagination — no visions superimposed.

A loud clang and bump told her the wheels had lowered. The noise lessened as the engines slowed, and Susan waited with tense anticipation until the first and then second wheel touched down. Engines roared as the jets reversed, and the plane taxied toward the gate.

Collecting her belongings, she felt oddly detached from her surroundings. She found her compact in her purse and looked into the small mirror at a stranger mechanically smoothing her hair. Nervous as Susan was, she had difficulty mobilizing herself. The aisle was already crowded with passengers eager to deplane. Her legs felt like cement. Perhaps she'd been sitting too long. Finally, she worked herself into the stream of frenzied travelers.

"Have a good evening," a flight attendant said as Susan stepped from the plane.

She forced herself up the jetway leading to the terminal. Looking around for Bill and Clare and not seeing them, she headed for the escalator and the baggage area. Maybe Carl had called and told them, she thought, and they're mad at me. Not spotting Bill, she stepped outside.

"Mother," Bill called from the other side of his small red MG convertible. Unbelievably relieved, she started to cry. Bill opened the passenger door as he brushed her cheek with a light kiss. "Miss me that much?" he joked.

She wiped her tears and thought how handsome he looked in his light-colored suit and new haircut that tamed his scraggly blond hair, now so neat and clean.

"Sorry I'm late."
"Where's Clare?"

"She has a final exam tomorrow in accounting. She's at the library, sends her love. She was sorry to miss you — hopes you'll stop on your way back home."

"Oh, I understand," Susan said. "Good for her. I hope you weren't too busy."

"I've been working a lot of nights lately, but it's good to get away. We're going to eat in that nice restaurant on the other side of the airport." Bill swung his little sports car out and around all the waiting taxis. "Like my car?" he asked, pulling up before an elegant canopied entrance. A uniformed doorman opened her car door.

"Hmm, you have good taste, Bill, in cars and restaurants."

Once inside and seated, Susan felt more relaxed, less detached — maybe it was the subtle lighting.

"I guess they keep it dark in here so you can't read the prices," Bill joked. "By the way, this is on me. I've never been here before, but it has a good reputation. Now what's with going to Arizona, Mother?"

"I'm meeting Aunt Lue for a little vacation. There's both a golf and a tennis camp. Lue likes tennis, and I love golf, so we should have fun."

"That's nice." Bill summoned the waiter with a practiced wave. "My mother has a plane to catch. We'd like to order, and, we'll have a drink while we wait for our food. What would you like, Mother? I guess I'll have the steak."

"I'll have the same and a vodka and tonic."

"White wine for me, Chardonnay," Bill said.

The waiter returned immediately, carefully centering their drinks on white scalloped coasters. Susan nervously twirled the thin red straw suspended in her cocktail.

"Well, Mother, how have you been? You look great."

Susan took a sip from her drink. "Dim lights help. But

thanks, Bill. You look terrific."

Bill smiled his half-smile, that smile she well knew when he felt uncomfortable. He shifted in his chair.

"I mean it, Bill. You look like a bona fide business man. You even look happy. Are you?"

Bill jutted his chin upward, a habit his dad had mastered. He lifted his broad shoulders, smiled and took a long swallow from his wine glass. "Yeah, sure. So how's Dad? Didn't he want to go play golf?"

Susan paused. "Remember last year, Bill, when I talked to you about how I felt about life, about my own life?"

Bill hesitated.

She could tell he was trying to remember, all the while thinking he doesn't want to hear this.

"Your father and I have separated." Her heart leapt to her throat as she watched him.

"You've what? I can't believe it. I suspected you were questioning some stuff, but not this — oh, no!"

"Bill," she said firmly. "I've left your father."

Bill shifted positions. He ran his fingers through his hair. He leaned both elbows on the table and cupped his chin in the palm of his hand. Slowly, he sipped his drink, looking off to the side. Finally, he looked at her, but she knew he was looking in front of her, in back of her, through her. Swirling the wine in his glass, staring straight ahead, he took a sip. He turned his head to the side and ran his finger around the contour of his ear. Then he picked up his fork between his first and second fingers and began to tap it slowly on the table.

Susan waited and felt sorry for him.

"Why didn't you tell me before?"

"Because I knew you'd say 'no.'" She waited to see if

he'd remember how she'd been there for him six years ago. Finally, she said, "I didn't want to put that responsibility on you. I didn't want to upset you."

"I'm upset."

"I know," she said, as if that would make everything all right.

The waiter returned with their salads. They watched him make room for the plates, pushing drinks and butter plates aside.

They withdrew into their silence, waiting for the other to speak. Candles flickered from white-clothed tables. Strident legs passed behind them. Voices, soft, now loud with laughter, floated above them.

From across the table, he reached for her hand. "I won't ask why," he said.

Susan relaxed to his touch. "Thank you."

The waiter served their meal. Silently, their eyes met, full of unspoken fears. They listened to resounding forks on china plates, knowing they had to eat, knowing there was a plane to catch.

SHADOWS

    I am almost awake after a fitful night. My hands grope about the bed as my mind swims through half-conscious sleep, struggling to remain in limbo, forget where I am. My fingers touch the cold chrome bars and recoil. I am still in my hospital bed, that same bed assigned to me less than a week ago.
    Smells have blended during the night to stale and antiseptic. The flurry of activity ending the late night shift has not yet begun, and the hall is quiet, but not quite. People cough, not a casual cough, mind you. These coughs resonate from unknown depths and resound through corridors into each door slightly ajar. Appropriate, I think. Why shouldn't we all share in what's relevant to the moment.
    This is the seventh-floor upper respiratory wing. At least that's how it's billed — 7 V U R for short — V for violet, color coded so no one will become disoriented within this huge maze and inadvertently end up in obstetrics where life flourishes. Mazes are popular now, but not for those of us who live in them caged within cold chrome bars from which hang life-saving devices. This is the lung-cancer wing. Odd name, wing, as though we could fly. A

couple of pneumonia and acute bronchial cases snuck in, but the rest of us landed here with lung cancer. We are either pre (like me), post, or in-operable (like Mary). No matter what they tell us, we are all moving rapidly toward the same ultimate experience.

Recently, I was running up to three miles a day. We spent Easter in Florida, and didn't I jog on the beach every day with the kids? They teased me and laughed when I fell behind, and I loved it when I finally caught up and collapsed on the beach in proud exhaustion. Not bad for fifty I had to tell them.

Hospital halls are strangely quiet, and I strain to sort out how all this started. If I can put everything in order, the whole crazy sequence might seem less like it's happening to me.

It begins with Mary. We quilted together each week. Along with five other friends, we stitched quilts for one another, like women did in the "old days." We laughed about that cliché at first. The quilting group soon took on an importance that surprised me. How often does a group of women work on a project, just for each other, not some unknown raffle-ticket winner.

I close my eyes, and there's my quilt, an adaptation of Grandmother's Flower Garden, a traditional pattern of colorful hexagons slightly larger than usual, stitched together to form flowers. A never-ending white path winds from one flower to another.

What day is it? I can't remember. Tuesday? We quilt on Tuesdays. Today the quilters will sit around a large wooden frame that stretches my quilt so they can all work at the same time. Except for the dress code, it's 50, 75, 100 years ago. Eyes cast downward, hands busied, words spill out easily. An unspoken law protects shared burdens from the outside world. Words shared over a quilt remain stitched within.

Within each puff of my "Grandmother's Flower Garden" there was a divorce, the death of a child, the frightening journey Mary took, and now me.

One day Mary came to quilting with the news that something unusual had shown up on her chest x-ray, and she was going to have a biopsy the next day. I dropped my needle. Mary fished through her sewing bag for another needle, then continued quilting as though she had just told us about a teacher's conference with her child.

We waited.

"I expect to stay in the hospital overnight," Mary said.

"I'm sure it will be nothing," I said. How could I have said that?

We all told her not to worry, and then one by one we recalled cases of people we'd heard about where everything had turned out ALL RIGHT. I knew I wasn't being honest. I really was worried. Why did I need to give her false encouragement?

#

Now suddenly I am with Mary sitting in her livingroom bay window after her biopsy. It is snowing. We are playing backgammon, and I feel uncomfortable, stilted. Words don't come.

"How was it?" I ask.

"Well," Mary shakes her dice over and over, "I wouldn't want to go through it again," and exposes the four-inch slit at the base of her throat made in order that all those miraculous scientific instruments could explore what was heretofore unknown to Mary.

I can tell Mary isn't going to volunteer any more information, and I can't stand it.

"Didn't they tell you anything more?"

"It's malignant," she says rolling the dice. "The problem is," Mary says moving her man across the board, "it's spread to the stem of the lung, so they can't operate." She raises her hand to her throat. "It's high-necked dresses and scarves for me. It hasn't spread anywhere else, though, and the doctor said that if I have to have a cancer cell, this is the best kind to have. I'm going to have radiation for the next few weeks."

I can't believe what I am hearing. I look closely at Mary. She studies her dice, planning her next move.

I want to say, "How could anyone have a 'best' cancer cell? Who are they kidding? Imagine that, Mary, you're dying with the best cancer cells available, straight from Saks Fifth Avenue, maybe? Is that what they've told you — with a straight face?"

Instead I say, "Hey, wait, you just won the roll. You've knocked me off the board."

#

Now it is almost 7 a.m., and I hear sounds reminding me that today's the day. My surgery is scheduled for 1 p.m. The morning nurse will be in soon to take my temperature and blood pressure. I will get nothing from the odiferous metal steam-table parked just inside the swinging doors by some white-garbed aide who ventures no further for fear of discovering first hand what's wrapped within this violet wing.

I can't keep Mary from sweeping back into my sick world. She pulls me along to join her, stranding me in corners I desperately want to avoid. Did Mary lie awake nights with the pit of her stomach tied in a knot? She never told me. Did she cry to think she would never see her kids get married — or have babies? Did she ever confide, "You know I won't be here next year at this time? What will you be doing without me?" Not to me she didn't.

\#

The quilters changed their hours of sewing to accommodate Mary's radiation treatments. Mary responded well to treatment at first and came to quilting each week reporting the tumor had shrunk. We never asked how she felt. We all pretended everything was normal. And even when Mary offered information, we said, "You're looking well," or "When will your treatment end?" as if the disease would truly end.

\#

I twist in my bed for all of us who lied. None of us had the nerve to ask the things we needed to know.

Mary went to see her parents in Arizona to play golf.

Returning home, she called, "Guess what? We're going ahead with plans to build the house. Isn't that great? I am so excited."

And so was I for her but puzzled since Mary and Bill had cancelled plans to build their dream house when Mary's illness surfaced. Perhaps Bill thought it would give Mary something to live for. At least it would fill her calendar. Now I know firsthand how awful it is to look at empty spaces on the calendar.

Meanwhile, I asked a doctor I knew who worked in oncology about Mary's prognosis, and he told me no matter what type cancer cell was involved, inoperable cancer meant three, six, perhaps twelve months. As it turned out, he hit it smack in the middle, six months.

At quilting, Mary projected her future about the new house. They were fixing a room on the first floor in case either of them became sick. When Mary wasn't around, we talked about how strong she was, how brave Mary and her family were.

Now I want to scream, "How phony we were! Why couldn't she, why can't we admit impending, inevitable death?"

#

I toss and turn from one chrome bar to the other.

#

While Mary was struggling to control the ever-increasing fluids in rebellion within her, I went for my routine health checkup. The next week I called the doctor's office expecting confirmation of my usual clean bill of health.

"We're sorry, Mrs. Emery," the nurse replied, "we can't give you a report on your chest x-ray because we haven't received it yet, but we've had a report from the radiologist that he's checking earlier x-rays. There's a shadow in the upper left lung. We'll call you."

Her words hung in the air.

A few days passed without word. I called again and was told I needed another x-ray taken. Waiting for the results was endless, even though I was told any x-ray could show unusual shadows. I called the doctor's office a third time, and the nurse would say nothing except that the doctor wanted to talk to me.

Finally Dr. Hocker came on the phone. "It looks a little suspicious, Mrs. Emery. Both x-rays show the same shadow. I want to take some laminated films this week."

"What is it?" I asked desperately.

"I don't know. I want more information. I'll have the nurse set up an appointment for you."

He clicked off, and I thought of nothing else. I couldn't even concentrate to read a newspaper while waiting for my appointment. I even called a doctor friend to see what he thought, searching for some authority to tell me not to worry.

"Am I being silly?" I asked him.

"It could be nothing, but you should be concerned. It's either an infection, a tumor, or nothing. Doesn't help much, does it?"

I clung to the hope it was nothing. Telling my husband about it was hard, but then he never was one to worry unnecessarily, so I wasn't really surprised when he wasn't as alarmed as I was. Still I wanted him to be. He just sat back in his rocker and continued reading as if I'd described returning a dress I'd brought home on approval.

Usually when I have a problem I can't keep from talking about it, but I couldn't bring myself to discuss the spot on my lung. It loomed like a foreign shadow, grotesque.

#

Quilting day came, and I silently tried to stitch away my worries. Besides, the shadow might be nothing. I pondered my secret. Even though I didn't like Mary's being secretive, it was different with me. As long as no one else knew about it, it was not true. To the rest of the world this spot, hiding within me, did not exist, and I, like Mary, pretended nothing was there. I decided not to tell Mary about the shadow.

Mary held her own against the strangler within her chest until one day she called to say the doctor thought she had flu. One day of the flu stretched into two weeks, and then one day Mary went into the hospital where her doctor removed a cup of dark brown fluid from her diseased lungs and sent her home, saying she would feel much better.

I tried not to think about the spot on my own lung when Mary told me this, but my stomach churned, and I wondered if this was a sneak preview.

Unseasonably warm spring weather arrived, so Mary and I arranged a few holes of golf. I watched with horror the thickening in her ankles and feet, her lack of energy, her golf ball going only half as far as it used to, slicing off to the right. Mary spoke lightly of it, but it scared me.

I wanted her to tell me how it feels. Is it bad? Is it frightening to talk about dying? Oh, please, Mary — please talk to me.

Instead I said, "You'll get it back, Mary. You know the golf swing, it comes and goes, mostly goes."

Later in the month Mary came close to saying how she really felt. The doctor had put her back in the hospital to control the fluid building up in her arms and legs.

"I'm discouraged," she said. "I had such high hopes," and that was all she said.

Mary's family didn't admit her finality either. When I called the house her son said, "Mom's getting along great. She'll be home by the weekend, good as new."

#

It's 9 a.m., and I stretch my arms over my head, trying to relax. The nurse comes in to shave my back. It feels marvelous as the razor skims off the rich lather, leaving me hairless, almost as good as having my back tickled. I *must* enjoy each sensual second for itself. I block out the horror of the future and just concentrate on how good this feels. I cast aside opaque unknowns for exquisite sensations that titillate. The nurse finishes much too soon, and I curl into a ball like a good girl and tuck my feet beneath the white gown that will take me through sterile halls, swinging doors, elevators and unknown rooms to cruel invasion.

Hard as I try to block out my future, I cannot stop the tormenting past and flash back to the day I had the second set of laminated x-rays. I lay on a hard table waiting for the team of technicians who finally reported that the shadow persisted and a whole series of laminations had to be taken.

That night I told my husband, "I'm really worried now." I turned from the sink to him. He sat reading his papers, pencil in hand, underlining important matters. I repeated, "The x-rays, Ken, I had to have more today."

"I wouldn't worry if I were you. It's probably nothing."

"Don't you wish," I said.

I knew he was trying to reassure me but in truth he was saying, "It can't happen to us." How indestructible we thought we were.

Mary went back into the hospital but returned home sicker. I made her soup, and we played backgammon and waited. Mary waited for the ever darkening shadow on her horizon, and I waited for the diagnosis of the shadow in my chest.

Two days before my diagnostic appointment, Mary went into the hospital never to leave. She begged her husband to take her to get her hair done that Saturday morning on the way to the hospital. At the time it seemed silly to me, but I can't fault Mary for wanting to look better. Perhaps vanity is baked so deeply within us that getting the hair done becomes the frosting guaranteed to make us feel good all over.

It was Ken's birthday the day I finally had my doctor's appointment. I stopped in to see Mary on the way to my appointment. I was shocked at how much she had changed in such a short time. Her face was lifeless gray, and her legs were so large and full of fluid she could no longer lift them. She asked me to shift her position on the bed. She was sleeping most of the time, and her eyes hung in their sockets, heavy and dull.

Oh, God, please don't let this happen to me.

We were silent for a time, and then Mary finally asked if I would do her a favor. "Will you see that my husband doesn't have a heart attack in the next few weeks?" Her words lacked heart and had a ring of submission.

I left her to sleep. Those were her only words concerning the finality of her world. I felt cheated.

After leaving Mary I headed for my doctor's appointment. Immediately upon locking the car, I realized I'd locked the keys inside and told myself to stay calm.

Once in the waiting room, I was hyper. At last a nurse ushered me into a room where x-rays attached to lighted boxes lined the walls. Transparent films exposed rib cages from every possible angle. They were meaningless until the doctor explained they were mine and pointed to a specific spot slightly whiter. I leaned closer to look and marveled how anyone had found it in the first place. It was circular, about one and one-half inches in diameter.

"Clearly, this concerns us," the doctor began. "It's a deep mid-lung lesion which means we cannot take a biopsy to determine exactly what it is. I recommend we remove the lung."

My body did not digest what my mind had just consumed. I felt no reaction. It was as though the lungs on the wall belonged to someone else.

"What do you think it is?"

"I think it's cancer," he said bluntly.

I stared at the innocuous shadow. It had somewhat of an artistic appeal. Then all at once, blood rushed madly through my body. I thought I might explode any minute and steadied myself against the wall.

"Can you get it all?" I finally asked.

The doctor laid his hand on my arm.

"We won't know until we operate and examine the lymph nodes to see if it's spread."

He went on to suggest a thoracic surgeon and explain what the operation would be like. Much as I wanted to know everything, I needed to be alone. I had to think about having cancer. I left the doctor's office feeling numb, having had the worst of my fears confirmed. I wished I could talk to Mary.

The parking-lot attendant was well equipped for emergencies, and I had no trouble getting into my car. Once alone, I sat buckled in my seat belt unable to move. Tears came faster and faster until I was sobbing uncontrollably. I bleated out the anguish I'd hidden so long, for me and for Mary. I even forced myself to cry harder, realizing what little control I had on my life that I had so carefully regulated.

"I don't want to die!" I screamed to no one.

On the way home I stopped to buy a cake mix and a present for Ken's birthday. By now I was a zombie except for periodic panic attacks when my stomach flipped, and the bizarre pronouncement regurgitated as a stark reality. Arriving home, I prepared Ken's birthday dinner as though I were someone else in my own kitchen.

When Ken arrived home he asked what the doctor had said, and I burst into a crying siege I could not control.

He comforted me. "Everything will be all right. You'll see."

Angrily, I turned on him. "All right? Don't you understand? The doctor says I have lung cancer. I know what that means even if you don't. At the most I have one, maybe two years to live."

I pounded my fists on the kitchen counter in desperation.

#

I am ashamed now to admit my lack of control, my angry words, but I must remember everything, sort out how I got here. It's almost 10 a.m. A nurse will be in soon to give me the shot into oblivion. Only a cartridge filled with chemicals plunged into my flesh that seeps into my blood and up to my brain can block out the horror that brought me here.

#

The same night of Ken's birthday I'd called my parents in Florida. I felt like a little girl again.

"Mom?" my throat choking so badly I had to stop talking.

The silence scared my mother. "What's the matter?"

I tried to control my voice. "I have a spot on my lung. The doctor says it's cancer, and I'm having an operation as soon as there's a hospital room available."

"Oh, no," she said. "We'll come, of course."

Always when I was little, my mother made being sick almost fun. In recent years, however, our roles have reversed. I've tried so hard to make them happy, and now I'm causing misery. The worst part of this whole mess is how sad and scared I'm making everyone. Did Mary feel this same agony when she looked at her family? Mary was silent and would remain so. I never saw her again.

Mary died leaving me wrapped in guilt, if for nothing more than because I'm alive, and she is dead. I don't want my family to feel guilty. I'll talk about it, the good and the bad.

Last week before entering the hospital was the hardest of all. I couldn't sleep, but every so often I'd slip into a surface doze from which the slightest noise would snap me back to reality, and then my mind would race crazily until I made myself get up.

The day after the doctor told me I had cancer I played in a tennis tournament that I'd signed up for long before. Two other women on the court had just been through messy divorces, suffering personal degradation that had obviously deflated their egos. At least my own self-esteem was not at stake, but that wasn't much of a trade-off considering the horrible knot in my stomach.

After the tournament, lunch was served in the club house, and I sat at a table with my partner. Suddenly I found myself pouring out what my doctor had told me, as if apologizing for not playing well. "You won't believe this, but my doctor just told me yesterday that he thinks I have lung cancer."

"You're kidding."

"Seriously."

"I am so sorry." There was an absurd silence. "Say," she nodded toward the entrance, "who is that girl that just walked in? Didn't we play against her in another tournament?"

I turned to look as others joined our table. Casual chatter bantered about until I thought I would burst. Hey, wait a minute, this isn't what's important. It's life, death, me. I excused myself from the table.

Life had become one long pitiful wait.

The following Sunday I entered the hospital. A battery of tests was ordered, and the operation was scheduled for Thursday. I felt one step closer to uncovering the mystery lodged within me. I wasn't completely convinced of the doctor's diagnosis. Somehow, I shouldn't allow it. The odds were nine to one in his favor, but he could be wrong.

#

It is approaching 11 a.m. I stare out the hospital window past all the essential mechanisms whirling atop multi-leveled roofs, past utility wires, beyond civilization and strain to see as far as I can. I settle way out there, far removed, and turn to look back on myself. The world seems such a drag. I'm losing the urge to fight. It's much less formidable out here on this cloud. I feel differently about dying here where it's soft and cozy. The anger, the sobbing sadness, the fear are gone. Smoothness eases its way through my fractured emotions, and something tells me it will be all right — whether I live or die.

Death must be good. Did Mary know this? I want to relish it like other natural functions that feel good. I hope I have time to feel where I am, savor the passage from being to not being.

A nurse arrives, pre-surgical medicine time.

I ask, "Is this the 'I don't care' shot?"

The nurse smiles and looks at her watch. "Everything's on schedule. Surgery will be coming to get you in an hour. Your family will stay with you until you go up." She pats my hand. "Good luck. I'll be here when you get back."

My eyes cling to her reassuring look.

My family walks into the room. It's comforting to see them all together, but how can I tell them it's going to be all right with me, even if I die.

The shot is taking effect, and I can only think, not speak. I listen to them talk. I feel like I am smiling and I think I ask, "Am I smiling?" I hear a phone ring in the distance, and I must have told someone to answer it because Ken picks up my hand and says, "It's ringing in another room." I try to open my eyes, but they feel so heavy.

I barely make out the orderlies dressed all in white. They transfer me to a cart with wheels. Thoughts race through my clouded brain. I see wheels, white wheels rolling. The family follows me to the elevator and silently stands guard. The elevator door opens. They wheel me inside and turn the cart so I can see my son, his wife, my two daughters, Ken, my mother and father. No one speaks. They look so frightened. Are they holding back their tears until the elevator doors close? Where are those appropriate words? I must tell them, but I can't, as Mary couldn't, and they will never know I'm no longer frightened, that no matter what, it's all right, that I know their love, and it is enough.

#

"Is she awake?" Ken asks.

"She can hear you. She's conscious," a nurse responds.

Inwardly, I shake my brain to sort out what I am hearing. I feel irritable. I open my eyes. The light is blinding, and instantly I shut them. It is too noisy. Amplified trains roar into Grand Central Station.

Ken calls into my ear. "Betsy, wake up."

I open my eyes again and try to raise my hand. Tubes invade me everywhere. Am I still being operated on?

The nurse reads my thoughts. "It's oxygen. You're in the recovery room."

Now I am more alert.

Ken is talking to me. "They got everything. It wasn't cancer. It was a fungus. Can you hear me? You're going to be all right. Do you understand? Everything's all right."

Slowly I lift my eyes to the nurse hovering above me. "Please — it hurts — so much!"

#

It is Tuesday. With eyes cast downward, hands busied, we stretch a new quilt.

HOOKED

A fish jumps behind me. Quickly I lay aside my pole and row toward the sound now transformed into circles enlarging on the water's silver surface. Only a big bass could make a splash like that.

Within a split second the line sings from my reel and snaps. Dropping the oars, I grab my pole in a futile reflex action. The line goes limp. I have lost the fish.

"Damn," I say. I know better than to lay a pole flat across the boat seats. I know a strike would break the line. It's a costly mistake, and I'm devastated. For the next twenty minutes I watch the fish leap wildly, twisting and turning, desperate to shake loose the embedded barbed hooks. Heartsick, I see it emerge high into a triumphant arc. It is one hell of a bass.

Over and over it rises above the water, struggling to free itself. The enraged bass churns the glass-like bay into a ferocious whirlpool. Darkness is blackening into twilight silhouettes, and every time the bass emerges it looms larger and larger, appearing first one place, then another, as if leaving one area for another could release its tether. The leaps grow less frequent, the attempts more feeble. Finally the once glorious prize jumps no more, and the water becomes smooth as burnished black marble, once again mirroring vibrant sunset-colored clouds from above.

My spirits sink, for by this time I am convinced I've not only seen the largest fish I've ever lost, but have lost the largest bass I've ever seen. I make a few more casts, but my heart isn't in it. I motor back across the lake to tell my husband about the one that got away.

Actually, he's heard this story before. Initially, he acts bored, but comes to attention when I mention that his favorite black-mouse lure is still swimming around in the lake with a fish attached to it.

"At least it's no ordinary fish," I say defensively. "I was over in bass hole when it struck. Like a fool, I left my rod flat on the seat — I know what you're going to say, just listen. I mean he was huge. Seriously, I think it was one of the largest bass I've ever seen in this lake. I feel bad about losing your grandpa's black mouse."

If proof of an ancient lure's power ever was needed, Grandpa's mouse had it. Teeth marks embedded above, below, and aft confirmed its reputation beyond a doubt. This bait was infallible. That mouse had tricked many a fish by simply skimming the water's surface while some voracious bass swirled below ready to strike.

These two images, one very real above the water and the other vividly imagined, are what hook me on bass fishing. Anticipation of the two crashing together in an explosion as the predator abandons its environment to devour its prey mid-air has me addicted to sitting hour upon hour in a boat, no matter the weather.

The next morning I relive last night's encounter with the bass. "I even dreamt about it," I tell Ken.

"Did he get bigger?" he teases, so I shrug off the sarcasm and decide not to tell him any more.

Later in the morning we run into the Larsens from across the lake. Ken can hardly wait to relay my frustration, cut into my fishing reputation.

"Well, Beth did it again. She lost her biggest fish ever," Ken laughs. "It's remarkable how the fish in this lake grow in direct proportion to the number she loses."

I squirm as my credibility is questioned in front of the Larsens, the very people I taught to fish.

"Ha! Ha!" I say. Over the years I've shown them all, Ken included, my fishing techniques and even share my favorite holes with them.

"Where were you fishing?" Jean Larsen asks.

"In bass hole."

"The catch is — " I grimace at Ken's pun. "My favorite bait decided to stay with the fish. It's the black mouse Grandpa used for years."

"Oh, my, that IS sad — to lose a bait like that," Jean says. "As a matter of fact we're on our way to go fishing now. Want to come along, Beth?"

"Are you kidding? I've lost my appetite."

"For today," Ken says.

It is almost noon when the Larsens unexpectedly pull up at our dock.

"Yoo Hoo!" they call. "Beth."

It sounds important. I think they might have hit a good spot and are coming to get me. Instinctively I grab my gear and head for the lake. Jean holds up a fish for me to see.

I stop short.

"What the devil?" Ken says.

Jean holds the very fish I lost, still alive, complete with Grandpa's mouse still hooked in its mouth.

I am speechless.

"Would you believe it?" Jean laughs excitedly. "We were fishing about a half-mile north of bass hole, and my bait snagged some weeds. I reeled and reeled and finally in came this big mess of line and weeds. Your fish was tangled in the midst."

"Unbelievable. This lake is at least four square miles. To top it off you were the only people we told."

Grandpa's mouse looks no worse for the wear, but the fish is infinitely smaller than I remembered. "Uh, I think it shrunk."

"What does it weigh?" Ken asks.

I am afraid to hear.

"Three pounds," she says.

"Is that all?" I ask.

"That's a *good* smallmouth, Beth."

"She thought it was at least five pounds," Ken can hardly wait to say. "So much for the one that got away."

"Hey, wait a minute," I say. "What about the mouse that got away?"

Carefully Jean removes the bait from under the bass' hard lip and hands it to me.

"At least we got the mouse back," I say to Ken. "Thanks, Jean."

Examining it, I catch a sudden glint from its yellow-rimmed eye. Staring deep into the dark glass center I see the sun drop just below a pine-jagged horizon as the water turns from silver to quiet black. Slowly the mouse crawls its way across the water's surface tension, hesitantly, irresistibly, flaunting its tiny wake, anticipating the moment. Then from the deep a powerful energy erupts in an effort to capture the prey. Within a split second the captured mouse turns into the predator, and suddenly the bass becomes the prey. The role reversal results in a fierce explosion.

Meanwhile, I, the third party, a mere tool at the mercy of the situation, respond with wild exhilaration.

The moment ends. The picture fades, but not the memory etched indelibly in my brain. And then, as if I'm not humbled enough, this mite of a mouse winks at me.

"Well, Jean, aren't you going to give Beth her fish?" my husband asks.

Jean and I look at each other.

"Poor thing's been caught twice," Jean says sympathetically.

"I agree," I say, admitting defeat.

Gently, she lowers the fish into the water. It takes a moment to gain strength, but then the magnificent bass gains strength and slips away to safer depths.

"I think it's a wiser fish," Jean says.

"Wiser is right," I say. "That's one savvy bass — sure made a liar out of me."

I look down at Grandpa's mouse in the palm of my hand with new respect. Its braided tail is all but disintegrated. I nestle it comfortably back into my tackle box. "Welcome home," I whisper.

FOR BETTER OR WORSE

It was a perfect day for a wedding. It was even the perfect month — June. Doris searched for emotion in her daughter's face, nervousness, whatever. Julie glanced down at her skirt and smoothed a wrinkle. Her soft, dark hair fell across her face obscuring Doris' view.

Twisting to examine the back of her wedding dress, Julie asked, "Have you decided yet, Mother?"

Doris looked away and hesitated. "I, I just can't bring myself to."

"But why?" Julie asked, confronting her mother. "All you have to is stand there, smile, and say 'hello.'"

"I don't know why, Julie," she said. "I thought I was doing well just to be here."

Doris saw the bitter disappointment in Julie's face. Just being here was not enough.

"If only Daddy was alive."

That hurt, and Doris cringed because she knew her husband would never have appeared. She expects too much from me, Doris thought.

She put her hand on Julie's sleeve. The material felt smooth and soft beneath her fingers. She leaned forward and kissed Julie's cheek, more from habit than emotion. It struck her how similar the two surfaces felt, soft and vulnerable, both strangely nostalgic. The dress, her own wedding, Julie, the child.

"You look beautiful," Doris forced a smile and stepped back to admire her daughter. She did look superb. "I think I'd better go in the church now and sit down. It's almost 11 o'clock. Good luck, sweetheart."

Julie sighed, "I can use it, right?"

Doris hesitated at the door. "I love you," she said, but turned quickly away before Julie could see her beginning tears.

Peter offered an arm to his mother as she stumbled toward the chapel of the small church. "How's the bride?" he asked.

"She's fine, I think, just a little nervous."

Doris was shocked to see so many people in the church. She stared straight ahead, convinced her smile probably looked phony since she herself didn't know what she felt. Halfway down the aisle her head felt light, her legs weak. Tightening her grip on Peter's arm, she thought she'd never reach her seat, as though she'd been walking forever.

At last, she reached the front pew and sat down. "There must be at least seventy-five people here," she whispered to Peter. "I had no idea Julie sent out so many invitations."

A young man whom Doris had never seen before sat down at the organ and began to play a traditional Bach prelude. Familiar strains filled the church. She might well have been sitting in her own Presbyterian church back home. The music began to calm her, and she thought about Julie's first communion when a precious little girl walked shakily down the aisle, her long dark curls a stunning contrast against the new white dress. She'd seemed so innocent that Doris had wanted to cry. Julie was still vulnerable, Doris lamented, and prayed she was beyond all the crying.

She stared at the printed program Peter'd given her that described the celebration about to unite the young couple.

So this was Julie's surprise. Capital letters across the front said, "A CEREMONY OF COMMITMENT."

Doris opened the leaflet and slowly read the message printed on the left side:

> Julie and Diane wish to thank all of you who have by your presence helped to create a very special momentous celebration. Each of you has played a part in our separate lives. It is appropriate that you are here with us as we begin our new life together.
>
>   Our love and thanks to all,
>   Julie and Diane

Doris took a deep breath. Somehow it frightened her to see it in print, so definite, so open for all the world to see. Is this really necessary, she wondered. Couldn't they just live together? Without all this fanfare? I don't understand, and then she forced herself to say it like Julie had asked her to, if only to herself, "But I want to."

She'd been through all the tears, all the guilt. Oh no, not all through, there was still plenty left, hard as she tried to erase it. She wondered when everything had changed, when it all went wrong, but she mustn't think that way anymore. Julie would say, "It isn't *wrong*, Mother." But what if she'd been more aware, had little tea parties with Julie more often. Why hadn't she questioned Julie's inviting the same girl over, watched her more closely, provided counseling earlier before that fateful night in the parking lot?

They'd taken Julie's closest friend along on a family trip to Florida. Doris went to look for a book she'd left in the car and found them stretched out on the back seat, kissing. To this day, she couldn't allow herself to picture that night without a sickening panic grabbing her, wrenching her heart and stomach into one inextricable knot. Even now, she could hardly believe it had happened. Hadn't there always been plenty of boys around the house? Boys Julie had liked and they, her. She was always so popular.

Doris tried to concentrate on the music. But a more recent encounter invaded her thoughts. Homosexuality had come up during a discussion amongst other women on the vestry in her church.

"Isn't that sinning?" one woman had asked. "I mean, according to the Bible, isn't that going against what the Bible teaches?"

"It certainly is," another lady had chimed in.

"I don't think so. No," Doris had said defiantly, "it's not sinning," and then turned to walk away before anyone could respond.

Doris knew full well why she'd not gone on to say that her own daughter had made this choice. Not long before Doris had been forced to reveal Julie's lifestyle to another friend. The effect had been devastating. Her friend covered her face with her hands in horror and said, "Oh, GOD, Doris, you poor thing! I hope that never happens to me."

Doris blinked back tears that blurred the words she held in front of her. On the page opposite Julie and Diane's message, Doris read the order of service:

PROCESSIONAL

> OPENING WORDS AND INVITATION
> CONGREGATIONAL RESPONSE:
> By our presence we undertake the responsibility for supporting Diane and Julie in this relationship into which they are about to enter. We will rejoice in their happiness, support them in times of testing, offer them our patience and forgiveness when they make mistakes, and remember them in our prayers, seeking God's blessing on them.

Something in the first sentence clicked. Doris remembered what her own mother had said when she first mentioned Julie's wedding and invited her to come.

"I want to support Julie emotionally, darling, you know that, but if I come to a — well — wedding, then I'm actually approving of what she's doing, aren't I?" There was a long pause. "I can't do that," she added. Then she had said, "I'm sorry, dear," before hanging up, leaving Doris staring into an abyss of hopes, values, all hopelessly tangled.

She returned to the moment as Peter slid into the seat beside her. He smiled and gave her an affectionate nudge. This must be hard on Peter, too, Doris thought, although he's the one who's been so supportive of Julie. But then, he'd been away from home at school and working in Boston. He didn't have to live with it like Doris did.

Looking around, she noticed some of her husband's relatives were here. Hers were not. At least his folks were here, not obviously missing, she thought bitterly.

The prelude ended. A penetrating silence followed. People shifted uncomfortably in their seats. Some coughed nervously.

Suddenly a loud trumpet fanfare announced the processional, and everyone turned to look up the center aisle, but the center aisle was empty. The two women had separated at the back of the church, and each walked alone down the outer aisle on either side of the church. Each wore a white full-length wedding dress and carried identical bridal bouquets of small white flowers. A spray of Baby's Breath crowned each head. They smiled and walked with noticeable pride and dignity. Doris was overcome. Trumpets heralded their march toward the church altar, toward this ceremony of commitment.

Doris shivered. How alone they are, she thought, how terribly alone. I feel so lonely for them. She had such an ache inside her to think her daughter had chosen this. What a risk she was taking, all the gossipy criticism, the rejection, let alone the vulgar chiding Julie had described. Recently someone had yelled "Dyke" for everyone to hear when Julie rode her bike home from work.

The minister stepped forward, facing the two women, and with raised arms invited all to stand. Together, everyone recited their dedication to Julie and Diane. The sound engulfed Doris. She mouthed the words, but silence emerged. Next came THE VOWS OF HOLY UNION. Doris held her breath.

Julie and Diane turned slightly toward each other, still facing the minister. Doris could not take her eyes from her daughter's face. Mesmerized, she saw Julie could not have hidden her sublime look even if she'd tried. Julie was smiling as Doris had never seen her smile before. The couple had not memorized their vows, but repeated after the minister, just as Doris remembered those same words when she and Mike had married.

"I, Julie, take thee, Diane, for my lifetime partner, to

have and to hold, for better or for worse..."

Suddenly Doris no longer pitied them. They had walked alone down separate aisles to stand together in a union that symbolized tremendous courage and dedication to each other. To her surprise Doris admired them — no, it was more than that — she was in awe. Her skin tingled with an elation she sensed in them, a culmination of their struggle to be honest and ring true, but most of all, to be taken seriously and belong to each other.

After the ceremony, Doris hesitated a moment in the foyer as Peter moved outside to greet his father's relatives. Suddenly, she could not face all the people. If only Mike were alive. Nothing had turned out like she'd planned.

She stepped back into the chapel. Why couldn't my relatives have come to the wedding — if only to be with me even if they didn't approve? Her mother's resolute words echoed in her ears and resounded in the empty sanctuary. "I can't take that responsibility, Doris, of approving, that's all. It's a fine line, I know, but I simply cannot cross it."

How simply her mother had figured it out. It was one side or the other, no middle ground to negotiate.

Doris walked back into the foyer. Julie and Diane maneuvered to find the right spot for their receiving line, a solitary twosome. She was reminded of Milton's last lines in *Paradise Lost* as Adam and Eve left the Garden of Eden:

They hand in hand with wandering steps and slow,
Through Eden took their solitary way.

Guests moved in from outdoors. Doris wound her way toward Julie and Diane to congratulate them.

She stepped in line between them and put an arm around each daughter.

LAST CHRISTMAS

Chris glances about at the boxes covering the living room floor, some filled, most empty. It's as though he's packing himself to be stored somewhere, in a crawl space, who knows. The dog whines as a squirrel scoots up the walnut tree out back.

"Hush, Jenny," Chris snaps.

The television drones on. Each evening Chris lip-syncs the day's news when Matt comes home from work. That's about all he accomplishes.

This morning he promised Matt he'd pack up all the Christmas ornaments. He stares at the glittering mish-mash pile in the center of the room. They should have put them into their boxes right when they took the tree down. It's important to be orderly. That pleases Matt, and it really *is* important. At some point everything must be put in order.

Each day it's harder for him to get up. Day by day he's weaker, hour by hour, more tired. Days are timeless — how ironic, he thinks, considering he hasn't much time left, like a self-winding watch on a dying man. If only he could finish this one job, he might feel some small sense of satisfaction.

Chris hadn't wanted tinsel on their tree. It caused an argument between them, but in the end Matt relented, just as he gave in when Chris wanted a real tree this year instead of the artificial one stored above the garage.

They were on their way home from the hospital after a particularly devastating chemotherapy treatment, hurrying to live normally before nausea set in. Chris spotted a lot filled with freshly cut Christmas trees. "Hey, let's get a live one this year." Matt drove on. Another lot came into view, and Chris looked pathetically at him. Matt slowed and pulled alongside the curb.

"Perfect tree," they said in unison when Matt propped it against the garage wall in a pail of water. "Damn, that smells good."

It snowed enough that week to be Christmas, but it didn't seem like Christmas until Matt walked into the living room barely able to maneuver the snow-laden tree into its holder. The pine unleashed an aroma unequaled in Chris' memory of Christmases. White lights, that's what he wanted. Matt, too, once Chris described the myriad effect against colored ornaments. Twice, no, three times he sent Matt out to buy more strings of white lights. He couldn't get his fill of the tiny exploding filaments giving life to each limb. Every surface shone and burst forth in all directions when he "turned on the tree."

"What if it turns brown," Chris fussed, "too much heat, too many lights?"

"You worry too much."

He looked to see if Matt was as cross with him as he sounded, but Matt smiled.

#

All that week, Chris turned off the tree lights whenever he left the room only to find that Matt had turned them back on. He was sure the needles would fall before they took the tree down. In the end they didn't. In fact, the tree hardly shed a needle until they undressed it, and Matt carried it outside.

Alongside the road, the naked tree rolled from side to side. Watching it whipped about by an unrelenting wind, Chris wished they'd bought a live tree with roots. They could have planted it in the backyard instead of tossing it in a ditch for a garbage truck to grind up. How could he have wanted a dead tree that looked alive? The artificial tree would have been better. They could have packed it away along with its ornaments, safely stored above the garage.

The lumbering sound of an engine forces Chris to right himself, pushing aside half-filled boxes of ornaments. Grabbing his cane, he limps once again toward the front door. He must see for himself their Christmas tree being loaded onto the refuse truck along with the Lewis' next door and others along the street, final as it will be. But it's just the UPS truck stopping next door. Tinsel still dangles from each limb of the Lewis' tree making it seem a little less forlorn than theirs. He shouldn't have argued against the tinsel. He wonders if Tina Lewis has had her baby yet. Would her husband call them as he had promised? Perhaps the truck is bringing something for the baby.

It is hard to think of birth when their tree looks so dead. Especially since he's dying — from the inside out. Everything inside him is shot to hell even if his outer shell is still unlined by age. Friends have stopped coming over.

All morning long, he keeps returning to look out front. Hobbling through the front hall, first toward the kitchen and then down the hall into their bedroom, he turns to look out one sidelight, then the other, as he passes the front door hoping the tree will be gone. With each trip, he thinks how patiently the tree lies, stripped of its adornment, waiting for disposal.

Exhausted, Chris finally flops into Matt's recliner. Just for a minute, he tells himself, then fixes his eyes on the huge forever green spruce tree in the backyard, each branch so familiar that they seem like family. Jenny jumps up, wriggling her way in beside him. He breathes a long, deep sigh. At least he accomplished one thing recently. He finished writing his funeral service, the liturgy, the whole bit, and even made plans for a wake at the funeral parlor. Matt won't have to face that. But he hadn't been able to imagine himself lying dead somewhere until he started packing those damned Christmas ornaments this morning.

He tries focusing on the thick, black tree trunk, wondering what goes on deep inside its dormant hulk. Is it rotting away from the inside when its outer cover still looks strong and healthy? He understands that. He'd learned to concentrate on a single object from the Franciscan Fathers when he was young. Just one thought — the tree — block out the rest of the world, leave nothing between himself and God. His adoration of St. Francis is permanent, that he knows, despite his disillusionment with the church. Disillusioned? Too soft a word — desertion is more like it. It's getting harder and harder to meditate, a communion he so desperately wants during this hellish ordeal. Looming larger and greater than his eyes can consume, the overwhelming tree suddenly becomes more than he can absorb.

Sobs convulse him.

"God, where *are* you?" Chris cries out in anguish. "You never warned me about *AIDS*!"

His doubt, his anger, slowly salve from pulsing agony to quiet submission.

#

He wakes in a sweat to a harsh mechanical sound. It's the disposal truck, and he struggles to get out of the recliner, then realizes it's the garage door opener.

"Hi!" Matt calls out, bursting into the house. "How was your day?"

Too tired to cry, Chris laughs.

"That good, eh?" and kicks aside a half-filled ornament box.

"I missed you," Chris says weakly, ashamed of not finishing his job.

"I guess *so*." Matt looks around at the mess.

"I'm a bastard. Go ahead, say it."

For a long moment, Matt's hands hang motionless at his sides. "No, you're not," he says. "I'll get it straightened up."

Too tired to resist, Chris watches each box top carefully secured on his last Christmas.

SILVER BELLS

Christmas Eve never changes — never enough time — late leaving the office — last-minute shopping. Arthur Bowles turns up his coat collar against a frosty wind and cuts through the parking lot toward the mall. "It's Christmas time in the city." Music spills into the street over a loudspeaker. Tricked by Christmas again, Art smiles to himself. Funny how one night can spin you back to a feeling you haven't known for a whole year. It settles in with a comfort. Right now he knows he will spend more than he planned.

"Soon it will be Christmas day," the music warns. He has one hour until the stores close. This year he'll buy Sally THE present, a real treasure. Once when he'd had a promotion he bought her a low-cut white evening gown. She outgrew it before it wore out. Made CEO of the company this year, he rides the elevator down from the top floor now. He'll find something she can't outgrow, or wear out, for that matter.

Nearby, a Salvation Army soldier stands religiously ringing his bell. Art reaches into his pocket for a coin and is about to drop it into the collection pot when someone bumps against him. He reaches out as the bell-ringer collapses in his arms.

"Quick, get help!" he shouts to a bystander and looks down at the pale, contorted face of the man in his arms.

"You'll be all right," Art says. "Help's coming."

Within a few minutes an ambulance arrives, and the stricken man is placed on a stretcher. Another Salvation Army officer hurries from the store and approaches Art.

"Please, watch the station for a minute," she pleads. "I must get my friend to the hospital. A replacement is on the way. God bless you!" Before Art has a chance to answer, the ambulance pulls away.

Dumbfounded, he looks up at the street corner clock. In less than an hour the stores will close. I'll still be all right if a replacement comes soon, he thinks.

Somehow he stands holding the Salvation Army soldier's bell. Clutching the black handle, he points the bell backwards, self-consciously hiding it, looking around for somewhere to get rid of it. The soldier's hat lies toppled upside down on the sidewalk. Art reaches down to pick it up when someone slaps him on the back.

My replacement, he thinks, only to look up into Bill Curry's open-mouthed face gaping at him.

"For God's sake, Art, what are you doing here?" belching a loud guffaw as he points to the bell and hat Art holds. "Early retirement?"

Before Art can answer, Bill claps him on the shoulder. "Gotta go, pal. Say, we're having a costume party New Year's Eve. Why don't you — ah — just come as you are? Hey, you could stand outside — greet the guests. Here," he digs deep into his pocket, "let me contribute to the cause." Still chuckling he leaves but not before dropping several coins in the pot.

Once again, Art stares up at the clock. Minutes are passing like seconds. Surely someone will show up soon. What would it matter if he left, probably not more than a few coins in there anyway. He could give the pot to a store clerk, but then no one would know where it was. The thought of carrying it with him seems ludicrous.

He abandons the idea of leaving and watches the passersby. Art stands taller than the rest. He can see way down the street. No one looks him in the eye. In fact, he's surprised how many go out of their way to avoid the collection pot. Instead, they look down with fixed stares, somehow avoiding one another, like bats with their inner radar.

An elderly couple pause to put coins in the slot. They smile approvingly, whether at him or their own benevolence he isn't sure. Surprised at the twinge of gratitude he feels, he smiles back as the two move on, slower than the others, causing hurried shoppers to change pace and circle around them.

A young woman steps briskly out of Hudson's, catches sight of him and puts a donation in the pot.

"Thank you," Art nods, not quite sure what to say.

"Merry Christmas," she says.

I should have said that, he thinks.

It's getting colder. A harsh wind whips in and around the buildings. Art moves from one foot to the other trying to stay warm, ringing his bell in time to *Jingle Bells*.

Suddenly, he sees Neil Jackson coming through the crowd. Great, he thinks, Neil can call the Salvation Army to send someone. Art grins as their eyes meet in recognition and is about to wave him over when a brief look of stifled embarrassment crosses Neil's face, and he turns to walk down the opposite side of the sidewalk.

"Damn him, anyway," Art murmurs. "He saw me."

Angered and hurt, Art grabs the Salvation Army cap he had neatly placed next to the collection pot, brushes it off, and settles it firmly on his head. Defiantly, he rings the bell. Several people give money. "Merry Christmas," Art calls to them.

He cannot believe this is happening. Except for Sally's signing him up to sell raffle tickets, he has never done anything remotely like this. He imagines the people who might benefit from the money being given. Seldom has he thought of them, for that matter. Except tonight as he left his office building, he saw that same ragged man he has seen night after night, stoically defending his corner, hauntingly destitute, very alone, no doubt in need. Art rings the bell louder.

He has almost forgotten the time as Mitzi Sherwood rushes through the crowd.

As though aghast at finding him here, she cries out, "Arthur, Arthur Bowles, does Sally know you're here? I just talked to her an hour ago, and she never mentioned a thing. Here — let me at least contribute something," handing Art her packages. "Last-minute stocking presents," she explains, fumbling through her purse. At last she produces a Neiman Marcus credit card and waves it in front of him.

"That won't work, Mitzi," Art says, purposely missing the humor.

"I guess not," she shrugs, "no petty cash. Gotta run," and takes off before he can explain.

Mitzi always irritated him at cocktail parties with her incessant questioning. Now he wanted to tell her why he's here, and she wouldn't listen. He feels cheated, and she didn't even give to the cause.

He continues to ring the bell, more slowly now, oblivious to all except his bell resounding to the Christmas music, interrupted by occasional coins clinking into the collection pot.

Finally, he spots a Salvation Army soldier winding his way through the shoppers. He takes the bell and hat from Art and steps into what a moment ago had been Art's space next to the kettle.

"We can't thank you enough," the man says to Art, politely dismissing him.

It is too late now to look for Sally's present. The stores will close in less than five minutes. Despondent, Art hesitates to move from the little station, to separate himself from this world he never knew before tonight. He shivers as a frigid gust of wind stings his face. A keen awareness overcomes him, and everything takes on the same wild importance. The air is as sharp and overwhelming as the Christmas lights that pierce the black night and the perfume sprayed on wrists passing through the revolving door. The replacement worker's bell rings deep into his brain. Exposed and estranged, Art feels as though he's suddenly shed himself. Not ready to lose the moment, he wonders now if he could have found the perfect present.

"Thanks again," the soldier says loudly. "You're a savior."

Art cringes at the praise.

He pauses a second, then asks, "Excuse me, sir, do you suppose I could buy that bell?"

The man looks surprised at the size of the bill Art holds. "Well — sure," he says. "Here, it's yours. I'm closing up anyway," and hands Art the bell.

Slowly Art moves into the stream of shoppers hastening home, his head bent forward, shielding his eyes from the

snow starting to fall.
He will wrap the bell for Sally.

DADDY'S GIRL

Julie's mind wandered as she stared out the window. A myriad of lakes emerged as the aircraft broke through the cloud cover. It seemed odd that these enticing blue splotches became non-existent once she was on the highway heading north from Orlando. She searched along the road, but their spaces had been absorbed — same as her parents who were tucked away within an abandoned orange grove in a created retirement community.

Uniformed guards waved her on as she eased the rental car over yellow humps built into the entrance drive. Security knew her well by now. The guards kept out sightseers and criminals, but they could not forestall the intrusion upon her mother's frail frame. *Community of Bliss,* the advertisement ironically promised. In truth, illness and death prevailed.

"She's awful sick, honey," her father said. "I think she may be going. You'd better come down." He'd put her mother in the hospital again. Actually, Julie didn't mind flying to Florida to help her father, inconvenient as it was to lay in frozen dinners for her husband and the kids, rearrange her schedule, see to having the plants watered, picking up the kids, all the while not knowing how long she'd be gone, not even annoyed that her older brother never came. Hadn't she always been *Daddy's girl*?

Her father waited in the drive as she pulled in front of the house.

"Thank God you're here," Carl said with relief. "The hospital has called twice — she's asking for me."

A neighbor lady waved from across the street. "Stop by and give me a report when you can. So glad you're here, Julie."

"Esther's been awful nice," Carl said.

Julie waved back trying to remember Esther.

On the way to the hospital Carl said, "Kathryn hemorrhaged again. She takes all those damn pills. I've just got to find out what she takes and when. This is the worst she's been — I want her home, Julie — " His voice cracked unable to continue.

"It'll be okay, Dad," Julie said trying to remain calm. She couldn't stand it when her father cried.

When Julie had first learned that Kathryn's condition was incurable, she hoped her mother would not linger, not suffer, so her father could get on with life, not support death. More than once, she'd been annoyed to find her mother so drearily stoic. Horrible as it was, she actually wanted Kathryn to die. Hadn't they both said aloud they hated to see her suffer.

"She wants so much to live," Carl said. It was that simple, and Julie knew then she would do anything to help her mother stay alive because her father wanted it so much. She would do this for her mother and the father she loved so much, but secretly, she needed to know how long this would go on. When *would* her mother die?

Kathryn slept once Carl and Julie were there. Julie

scanned a Hospice leaflet she found on the bedside table. Hospice could solve the problem of Carl's determination to bring Kathryn home and not put her in a nursing home. "I promised her," he said. Within the next few days, a hospital bed arrived at the house, and they brought Kathryn home.

The last time Julie had been here Kathryn had asked her point blank, "Do you think I'm going to die?" Julie had hesitated, searching for the right words, unsure of what her mother wanted to hear. "You're pretty sick, Mom."

"I don't want to live like this," Kathryn said with resolution.

"I know, Mom."

But she hadn't known because Kathryn's condition worsened, and Julie could see her mother wanted very much to live. Even though it hurt when they moved her, she still asked them to lift her to a chair and was even willing to use diapers.

Esther popped in and out each day, never staying too long, always praising Carl for his sympathy and concern. One day, as she was leaving, she pulled Julie aside, "Since losing my husband, I can't take a serious illness. It depresses me. I wish I could help with Kathryn, but I can't. Carl takes such good care of Kathryn, doesn't he, and keeps her so clean, but he needs you, Julie."

Julie smiled at the praise. "You're nice to stop in so often."

Kathryn liked Esther, or so she had said, but Julie had trouble believing that because Esther did not play bridge and besides she smoked. The main praise her mother had for Esther was that she kept a clean house. A clean house went a long way toward pleasing her mother, that and someone's eyes. "I just don't like her eyes, don't ask me why," her mother would say about someone. She must remember to look at Esther's eyes. Julie had never understood about judging a person by their eyes, but Kathryn could tell in a minute. So Julie caught herself looking deep into someone's eyes but never found any revelation about inner character like Kathryn did. Carl was less judgmental. He seldom announced his feelings for others, except where Julie was concerned. Theirs was a quiet understanding.

Julie and her father took turns checking on Kathryn at night. Nearly two weeks went by, and Kathryn's condition stabilized although she slept most of the time and seldom spoke. They fell into a familiar pattern of caring for her. Carl acted as though she would go on living forever, so sick yet alive. It unnerved Julie, as if they were selfishly keeping her alive, working off guilt for bad things they'd said but couldn't remember.

Julie knew she'd failed her mother, not often, nothing large, but it was inevitable she couldn't please Kathryn. They had few interests in common. Her mother would have loved for Julie to play bridge. Then there were the times she preferred playing golf with her father to some shopping spree.

"Why don't you get involved in some nice volunteer organization, like a garden club?" Kathryn once asked when Julie described her inner-city African-American women's group. There was no simple answer, nor did Kathryn seem to expect one.

Friends brought in food, but Julie cooked for Carl anyway, making his favorite dishes — milk gravy for his potatoes, buttered parsnips, sour-cream raisin pie. Esther stopped in often and raved about how wonderful Julie was to her father.

Julie decided to go back home once they had Hospice.

It was a comfort knowing someone would come in daily to bathe and check on Kathryn, knowing she wouldn't have to be hospitalized again. Hospice could handle any emergency, even death. Besides, Esther came over every day.

The day before Julie was to leave, and they had just finished lunch, Kathryn moaned. They hurried in to her.

"She just needs to know we are here," Carl said. They repositioned her. "You sleep now, Mommy," he said and tucked a blanket around her. "I'm going to take a little nap. Julie's here." Kathryn nodded like a child.

"Stay with her a few minutes, just till she settles down and falls asleep."

Julie sat in the rocker beside the bed, her hand resting on her mother's limp arm and stared outside. A grove of barren orange trees killed by last winter's freeze was framed in the window. Slowly, Julie kept the rocker going with a tap of her foot, consumed with how horrible it was to want to know when her mother was going to die, the sooner the better. How ironic that the Hospice doctor had already signed the death warrant. In writing her mother was legally dead as Julie watched her chest rise and fall with each labored breath.

Julie rocked back and forth, trying to ease the guilt from her mind. Her eye caught the rocker's motion in the glass of a picture behind her mother's bed. Together they were mirrored in a portrait of a little Julie seated on her mother's lap, the now superimposed on the past, except their roles were reversed.

The image dizzied her, and she closed her eyes, then looked up at her mother's shrouded form. Each night when she rubbed moisturizing lotion on her mother's cracked, dry skin, it reminded her of an ancient lacquered map of the Holy Land. Did she grease, salve her mother, so she could slip away more easily?

All along, Julie had supposed that one day she would receive a phone call from Carl telling her, between sobs, that her mother had died, and she knew she would be sad and would cry, but she was not prepared for it to drag on so long.

At least three times her father had thought Kathryn was dying, but she fooled them each time, and now Julie was trapped, watching her mother inch into that *other* world. Part of her was already there, Julie was sure of it, but stubbornly her mother kept sweeping back into this world of dead orange trees. In and out she slipped, much like when Julie sat in her little sandbox outside the back door, and Kathryn would peek out at her to see what was going on, see where Julie was.

Julie would be there for Carl, she wanted to cry out to her mother. Maybe then she would be content to leave them.

Suddenly a strange guttural noise frightened Julie. A trickle of blood oozed from the corner of Kathryn's mouth, staining the pillow. She'd never been here during previous hemorrhages. Carl was still asleep. She felt for Kathryn's pulse.

"Dad," she screamed. She shouldn't be the one to watch her mother's last breath.

Groggy from his nap, Carl stumbled into the room.

"What's wrong, honey?"

"She's hemorrhaging — I can't find her pulse. Should I call Hospice?"

"Oh, yes," said Carl. "Hurry! The number's right on the phone."

Julie found Carl kneeling beside Kathryn when she returned. "Is Mom — ?" She stopped mid-sentence.

"Poor Mommy," Carl whispered, brushing thin wisps of hair from Kathryn's motionless face. "Poor, poor Mommy," he repeated. "It's all over, Mommy, no more pain, no more, no more sickness," his voice trailed off as he stroked her. He didn't sob, but his tears fell onto Kathryn's face. "We cried together, didn't we, Mommy?" Gently, he wiped her face with his cheek.

Julie turned away from his anguish.

The doorbell rang, and Esther made her way to Kathryn's room before Julie could stop her.

Carl rose blindly. Esther put her arms about him. Julie couldn't believe what she was seeing. Carl was turning to Esther instead of her. Quickly, she stepped beside her father and slipped her arms around him, resting her head against his face as the two women embraced him.

All of Carl's pent-up emotions broke loose. "She's gone," he sobbed. "I can't *believe* it! We would have been married fifty years this Christmas."

Julie cried. Bent from the weight of his loss, he seemed smaller and older than usual. More than anything, she wanted to ease his pain.

"It's better for Mom, Dad. It's better now."

Carl nodded.

She'd convince him that it was better, that he'd be fine.

The next few days passed quickly with everyone stopping by while funeral arrangements were completed. Esther was especially kind. The family came and went. Neither Julie nor Carl slept well, but everything was attended to, even Kathryn's belongings. Julie saw to that. She put everything in bags and threw her mother's life into a Salvation Army dumpster.

Once the funeral was over, Julie assured herself that Carl would quickly adjust. After all, he had plenty of interests and knew how to take care of himself.

"You can cook, clean, do the wash, everything, Dad. Not many men can claim that. I'm so proud of you."

During the week they went over what he would do with his time after Julie left.

On the morning of Julie's departure Carl reassured her, "Don't worry about me. I'll play lots of golf, go to the rec house for bridge."

But Julie wanted to worry. "Don't be too stoic, Dad. Call me when you're lonesome. Promise you'll call when you get depressed. It won't be long until you fly up to see us for Christmas."

Carl gave her a reassuring pat.

"Besides," she warned, "you'll probably have to fight off the widows. If Esther is any indication, you'll get lots of invitations. Don't forget, Dad, there's safety in numbers."

"No question," he said.

They loaded her luggage into the car, and Carl disappeared momentarily around the corner of the house.

"Oh, Dad!" Julie choked as he approached with a bunch of his roses for her to take home. "They're beautiful."

They kissed goodbye. Overwhelmed by a wave of guilt about leaving him, she clung to him a moment longer than usual.

"We'll expect you for Christmas, Dad, and — I'll call you soon, like tonight."

"Now, now, don't count on me to come visit," Carl said. "I have to get used to being alone. Besides, you know I don't like to travel north in the winter."

Julie waved off his objections. "Don't be silly. We need you."

Esther walked over as Julie backed out the drive. Julie rolled down the car window.

"We'll take good care of him," Esther said. "Don't you worry."

"Thanks," Julie said, "you're a love."

As she drove off, she glanced into the rearview mirror. Carl wiped his eyes, then smiled at Esther. Tucking his handkerchief in his back pocket, he led Esther back to the house. Julie slowed to watch them. Something seemed different. She couldn't remember Carl ever taking her mother's arm quite that same way.

#

Julie waited anxiously as the phone rang several times before Esther answered.

"Where's Dad?" Julie cried. "What's happened?"

"He's right here," Esther answered. "We're just finishing supper. Your father's fine," then giggled, "right, Carl?" Julie could hear Carl chuckling in the background.

"Tell her I'm fine," Carl echoed.

"Uh — well, I won't bother him then. I just called to say I got home okay." Julie paused. "Tell him the roses look great on our hall table."

"I certainly will," and Esther repeated the message to Carl. "He says, 'That's swell.' We'll call you soon, Julie," Esther said and hung up.

Stunned, Julie stared into the dead phone. A smiling Carl and giggling Esther seated across from each other at her mother's kitchen table loomed large.

THE END OF PAINTING

"Where does it end?" I ask the guard.

He shrugs.

They call it a retrospective, sounds big. Enormous. I should go through this whole thing backwards, but the guard directs me to start at the beginning. Why call it a retrospective? They should use another word.

"I'm certainly not about to start where the artist began the work if it's called a retrospective," I say firmly. "How often do I get the chance to go backward in time?"

He looks at his watch.

I plant my feet. "I want to start at the end."

He calls a co-worker. "Against the flow," I overhear.

"Work my way through to the beginning," I counter.

I've paid for my way, not direction.

The idea of a retrospective, to start at the end of creativity and weave backwards is intriguing, makes sense. Oh, I will say to myself, the artist did this *after* what I will see next, not knowing what comes next when in reality it was before. Know the end before the beginning, see the results of creation before it began.

#

"Think back on what you've done," the mother said. "Shame on you."
#
The couple behind me listen to my protest. I see them nod in approval.

"We want to start at the end, too," the woman says.

"Not afraid of being trampled?"

We shake our heads no in unison.

I smile, momentarily connecting to them.

Some minutes later the three of us are led directly to the retrospective's exit to begin the exhibit.

"Enjoy yourselves," we are told.
#
"Don't look back," the coach said.
#
The couple break from me. I'm relieved to be alone, to digest a creative world in retrospect, ruminate in reverse.

Suddenly the mild-mannered twosome become vocal.

"You got us into this," the man says.

"Shut up," the woman whispers between clenched teeth. "This place echoes."

"Never contented," the man says. "This is ridiculous."

"Darling, please. Let's be pleasant."

"Oh, now it's 'darling,' is it? Since when?" the man asks.
#
I hang back. Let them stampede. These people don't belong here. I yearn to absorb abstract expressionism on my own, without their barbed words.
#
"Words are destructive," the husband said withdrawing before she'd finished. She strained to remember what she'd said.

#

But these two are not to be rushed.

"Look at this," the man says. "The artist painted this just two years ago. Where were we, darling," he asks, "at this time that year?"

The woman bends forward in an exaggerated fashion to read the written description next to the painting. "1994," the woman says. "You were still involved."

"Involved?" his voice heightens. "With your in-laws, that's what, up to my ears."

"Up to your ass if you recall, darling, and not with your in-laws."

#

Stop it, I want to cry out to these amateur voyeurs, art is supposed to lift us above all this.

#

"Why would one want to paint?" the husband asked.
"Let alone write!" she screamed back.

#

"All in your imagination," the man exclaims flatly, walking toward a large green and white painting that covers most of one wall. "Come here," he demands. "Now what do you see?"

"Body fluids. What year was it?" the woman asks.

"1992. Does it matter? Enjoy it for what it is."

"1992!" she screams.

I look nervously about for guards.

"When I think about what you were doing in 1992 — your little cunt was calling the house every other day."

"Spare me," the man wails directing her into the next gallery.

#

I stop in front of the massive green and white canvas. I

see no adultery, no fornication, no lying. What did they see to provoke such emotion? Perhaps the green forms are sexual, phallic symbols? I don't see it. I look more closely. What enchants me are the spaces, white spaces between green lines, curlicues that know no bounds, spiraling off the canvas into space. Axial lines crisscross as a flat counterpoint. This painting has been distilled to bare essentials, to what is truly important, ethereal motion.

#

The couple has not made it into the next gallery. They are affixed in the doorway.

"So what did you think it really meant?" the woman confronts him, hands on hips, refusing to move.

"Freedom," the man says.

"Is that all you think about? I might have known. Your nasty green freedom!" and she stomps into the next gallery, but not before shouting, "You and your body fluids!"

The man follows along and takes the woman's arm. They stand surprisingly complacent before a group of paintings along a side wall. Suddenly the man and woman have become contented art-gallery kittens, perhaps absorbed within a few private moments they normally don't find in a busy commercial life that involves earning a living and feeding themselves. Irritations miraculously subdued as though never erupted, the two walk through the room, arm in arm, quietly gazing from one oil painting to the next.

#

"Don't look back," the coach warned.
Properly warned, she looked down. "Oh, my God."
"Look up," he commanded.

#

Are these paintings becoming better the farther back in

time they go? I thought things were supposed to improve with age.

#

"You've changed," the husband snarled.
"I can't help it," she sobbed. "I've aged."

#

The couple move on.

They stop before a large painting. It is filled with bright colorful lines, many of which dissect each other. Some fly off the canvas.

"This is destructive," the woman says grabbing the man's arm. "These paintings are destroying me."

"How can you say that?" the man asks. "I like them. They are stimulating."

"They leap out at me. The lines, those arrows, the daggers. I can't look." She hides her face in her hands. "Out to get me."

"It's your imagination, dear," the man says. "I don't see that. Let's move on, please."

"You mean backwards," the woman corrects him.

"That was your idea," he reminds her.

#

Why don't you conform – like the others? the husband silently demanded.

What others? I wanted to ask. I don't know them. Were they before me?

#

I stop and face a painting the couple has skipped. How foolish of them, I think. They have no business here. This painting says it all. It's almost pure white. I'm mesmerized. But of course it's not pure white. The longer I stare, the more colors I see, soft, calming nuances of ribbons. Would the woman ahead have seen daggers, swords? The

quietness on the canvas refreshes me.
#
"I'm tired," the woman complains.

"Of course, darling, I've hurried you."

The woman slumps on a bench in the middle of the room and stares blankly at another painting. "Christ!" she says suddenly reviving, "What does this mean?" and points to the painting before them. "These are just details, silly fragments. Someone's erased everything." The woman turns away in disgust.

"This is abstract expression, my dear."

"It means nothing to me. I want all or nothing."

"You've always been self-centered," the man says softly, "a bit selfish, I'd say. Center stage and all that."

"You're the exhibitionist," the woman says loudly.

"Let's move on," the man snarls.

"We're not moving on," she insists, "we're receding."

"Have it your way."

"Very funny." The woman laughs raucously, throwing her head back. "The exhibitionist in the exhibit."
#
I cannot believe the drama I am watching. I hadn't signed on for performance art.
#
"Talk to me," I begged the husband afterward.
#
"Where do you think an artist gets all these kooky ideas?" the woman asks.

"Artists do not paint with ideas, my dear."

"Just where do you think all this comes from?" The woman sweeps an arm wildly about the room. "Tell me," she confronts him, "what do they do to create this crap?"

"They use paint, my dear."

"Don't defy me," the mother said or was it the husband.

#

Scattered patrons drift in our direction and stare at us headed the wrong way. They meander, hiding behind whispering cupped hands.

"I like this," the woman suddenly declares, separating herself from the man.

He joins her before a miasma of color.

"Why?" the man asks.

"It reminds me of your father's second marriage."

"The bitch," he murmurs.

"Not as bitchy as your mother," the woman says.

"You enjoyed that wedding?"

"Yes, yes, I did," the woman says sounding more adamant as she speaks. "It was colorful."

"If you call drunkenness colorful, then yes, I agree."

"See that blue?" the woman continues. "The sky was *that* blue. Look over here." She approaches the painting and touches the left side of the picture. "This is where you and I stood. I remember pretending we were saying our vows all over again." She looks up at him. "For the first time."

Within seconds a guard appears. "You are not allowed to touch the paintings, Madam," he growls. "Mind the line," and he points to a white strip shouting from the floor.

"The nerve," the woman says glowering.

"Go on, my dear, what else do you see?"

"A family." She gestures just short of touching the painting. "See this conglomeration? That's togetherness."

The man cocks his head.

The two link elbows and continue on their way to ob-

serve more paintings.
#
They saw a wedding? I ponder in front of the colorful rendering. I have trouble getting back into my mindset. Their voices intrude.

I see confusion, disorder. These people have influenced my conception, usurped my reaction. I applaud 'cup of the hand' whispers. I need to move on, find something I can confront on my own, not enter an arena already brainwashed.
#
The judge pounded his gavel. Divorce concluded. She didn't faint, but an array of many colors passed before her.
#
I walk toward a gallery that lurks before me, quite different from what I've seen thus far. I hurry to find where I stand in this artist's life. I have come half-way, not toward the death of the artist's creative world, but approaching its birth. The thought turns me on. It seems electric the closer I get to what I sense will be the apex of this painter's world. What should I look for? What will an artistic crisis look like? Will I recognize an epiphany? I expect a change, a place where sudden transformation will surmount. Something documented.

The next room astounds me. I am not sure why. My pace slows, and suddenly I'm struck by a new thought. The image of a woman on canvas enters through my eyes. It transforms within my brain to an impression, a feeling, a thought and finally words. So what happens when the written word enters my brain? The word transforms into an image, I know that, a picture, the opposite of the image I've just received which becomes the word. But what happens when the two meet mid-brain? Do they pass, backs turned, unwilling to honor the connection — not admit that ideas are resolved to images and images transform to ideas? Or do they collide and do battle and does the more powerful win? I suspect a continual confrontation, but that doesn't tell me who wins.

In this gallery a myriad of female images emerge before me on one canvas after another. Forms that moments ago were lines, arrows, daggers, no — that's not true. I saw spaces, spaces between vibrant colors. Now I see raw humanity.

The couple before me moves into the next gallery. I savor being alone but cannot resist sneaking up on them, like a sleuth.

The woman sits down and closes her eyes. "Look at that painting. Now," she says folding her hands as though praying for salvation, "tell me a story."

"A story?" he asks.

"Yes, I want a bedtime story."

"Hmm," he says and clears his throat. "When I was young my sister hated me."

"Is the picture dictating to you, or are you just making this all up?"

"No, no, the painting is what's made me think of it."

"Oh, all right then, go ahead." She continues to hide her eyes. "I will look when you're finished."

"Wait," he says and moves closer to see the date the picture was painted. "Okay," he says, "right on target," and sits back down beside the woman.

"It was my birthday, my 10th," he continues. "Mamma had planned a party for me with the family. Actually it was a Sunday picnic, but she'd told everyone to bring a record because she and my father were giving me a record player for my birthday. It was a big deal because we didn't have a

record player in the house. We didn't even have TV!"
"Oh, my God," the woman said. "I knew you were underprivileged, but not destitute."
"Actually, I don't remember missing out. It was kind of fun to think about when we would get one."
"Wait," the woman says still blindfolding herself. "What do you see in the painting that reminds you of all this?"
"Well, I see what looks sort of like a candle."
"Are you sure it's not a disguised penis?" the woman giggles.
"Shh, do you want to hear the story or not?"
"Yes, a bedtime story," she says, her face still concealed in her hand.
People pass in the opposite direction, look at the woman and turn away, perhaps too embarrassed to intrude on a scene not committed to a canvas, afraid of the moment.
"I see the picnic table," the man continues. "Something looks like presents, under wrap."
"What's that got to do with your sister?"
"Shut up, one thing leads to another." He pats her thigh. "I haven't gotten to that part yet." He stops and studies the painting. "We pick the perfect location, you know how it goes, a table near the toilets, yet close to the swings and teeter-totter, far enough away from others so we feel like it's our own place. That's real important, like we'd just walked out our back door."
"What's in there about your sister?"
"You in a hurry, gotta go the toilet or something?" he snaps.
"No."
"I'll get to it." He contemplates the painting before

him. "I wish you'd look. There's a section I don't understand. It doesn't fit with the other shapes."

"What color is it?" she asks still not peeking.

"You know that rainbow ice cream you like, the kind that makes me sick?"

She nods.

"There, in the upper right corner, I hate it yet like it. The brilliant color is heavy. I see now, it's falling, this rainbow glob is about to demolish everything below it."

"I can't stand the suspense," the woman squeals, still not looking, and tries to stand. The man pulls her down with a plop onto the bench.

\#

I listen and watch, as much a part of the scene as the picture that has them trapped.

\#

Stop watching, the husband said.

\#

"What about the sister?" the woman asks frantically.

"She went off to explore shortly after we arrived, too old for all that nonsense. No one noticed for a long time. Even when I opened the flat presents all the same shape. That was directly after I opened the record player. 'Wow,' I said. 'Where's Sis? She'd die to have this record player.' I looked around for her, hoping not to see her, so glad to own something she would want. I could hold it over her." He stopped. "Just like that rainbow up in the corner, suspended, ready to drop any minute, annihilate whatever is below. I wanted to annihilate her."

\#

I cannot help myself. I float into their gallery and sit on a bench directly behind them.

\#

"A rainbow can do all that?" the woman asks. "Rainbows are supposed to bring happiness."

"Look and see for yourself," the man says.

"Oh, no, I couldn't stand it. Is there a pot of gold?"

"Not that I can see."

#

Annihilate? I survey the painting. Certainly the colorful grouping at the top right is threatening, I have to agree. But what about the rest? I'm open to suggestion. The color is effective. It leads my eye up and off the canvas. I don't see this as oppressive. These people know nothing about art. I cannot stop listening.

#

"Go on," the woman prods.

"After all the records were unwrapped, we looked around for my sister," the man says.

"Wasn't your mother frantic by this time?" the woman asks.

"No, not yet."

#

"Peeping Tom, that's what," the mother shouted. "You encouraged him."

#

"We went ahead and ate the cake, without her," the man says still staring at the painting. "Afterward someone said there was a scream."

"So?" she says grabbing his crotch.

"Ouch!"

"The story," the woman begs.

"We caught the man," the man says, "my dad did. Well, not exactly a man. He was a kid. I'd never seen him, but my sister said he'd raped her."

"Of course, she was attacked," the woman says.

The man sits silently for a moment. "She ruined my birthday. I've never liked her since."

"This is your idea of a bedtime story?"

The man smiles and places her hand on his groin.

"You're sick!" she screams with delight.

"Look for yourself now," the man says.

The woman uncovers her eyes, blinks several times and stares at the painting before her. "I think you had a very nice day for your party," she says and stands up to proceed. The woman hesitates a moment, looks back at the painting and shakes her head. "What's with those folds that loop? Needs some organizing."

#

My concentration destroyed, I look at the painting again and slump. Why would people of this caliber even want to come to an art museum, let alone a sophisticated exhibition like this? They know nothing about art, what it's supposed to convey, what came before that inspired the artist to paint this way. They have no interest in what the artist is saying, no sense of psychological inner space on canvas. I'm so distracted, neither do I. I rise and drag myself along behind them like a tethered dog.

#

"Looking back, what have you to show for yourself?" the mother asked.

"Just what did you spend your day doing?" the husband asked.

#

"I like your sister," the woman says.

"Notice how the shapes are becoming recognizable," the man says.

"And more colorful," the woman adds.

"Now that we've come to the end."

"You forget," the woman coos, "we've gone back to the beginning."

"I like it here in the beginning." He puts his arm around the woman. He points. "There's a tree."

"And a fence." The woman smiles.

"A house."

"A dog."

He plants a kiss.

The couple move toward the entrance to leave. The woman turns and waves to me, "Bye, nice to meetcha."

I smile feebly.

#

"Remember the past to know the future," the teacher said.

#

I've tired with beginnings, vacant explicit explanations. Drained, I stand before the painting vacated by the couple. Its realism disappoints me. The unimagined bores me. It is dreadful to regress into what's been. A mistake, a horrible ending to a bad beginning. I'm as angry stationed before the obvious as the couple was with nuanced flickerings.

A sudden stream of visitors pushes its way to begin the exhibit. I am thrust headlong on the crest of their enthusiasm, unwilling at first to move forward, then suddenly quite content to suffer the tide.

Swept along, I harvest loose fragments, savor ribbons that float from canvas to canvas, no more slip-knot warnings to tighten and strangle. Disarmed, I stand watch over foaming pillowed whites — quiver before dismantled rainbows.

HAPPY HOUR

I've always tried to please you. My God, how I tried.
You have! You HAVE!
Which? Try? Please you? Oh, never mind. Now that it's over, it doesn't matter if I succeeded, does it? Success at its worst is maddeningly subjective, at its best, frighteningly fleeting. At least I did my job as far as I'm concerned. I think I sacrificed enough — didn't I? Gave you enough? Of me, that is, didn't I?
Oh, yes. Oh, yes, you did. You did.
I wish I were you.
Why?
So I could see myself. I wish I could sit there where you are, be you — see myself.
You might not like it.
Oh, I don't mean see me as you see me, I want to see for myself — I would see me — only I would be you, do you understand?
Sheri, what's happened to you?
You're right. Whatever it is, it's happened TO me. But in reality, it's what hasn't happened to me. Isn't that funny? What is it they say: to, for, and by the republic?

❖ LOVE TAKES

It's the "by" that interests me.

I never thought of your having political interests.

I don't. It's history that captivates me — in its mesh of whoever staggered before me. I'm as incorrigible as those foundering before me — I respond like a sheep following its mirrored swagging tail. Call to me, and I'll fall in line. Put some yapping dog at my heels, and I'll yield and turn. Bring on the shepherd — I'll fall peacefully asleep.

And you'd consider yourself a success, be content then?

Perhaps, but enter the wily fox, the slinking yet overpowering wolf — now to the test: will I recognize the predator, having been so cleverly seduced by its predecessor? Here history replays its ritualistic role.

My dear, your whining bores me.

I can understand. It brings me to tears. Have I bored you to tears yet?

SUBURBAN SANTAS

"Christmas!" Marion collapsed on the bed.
Joe smiled. "Christmas is a long way off."
"The stores don't think so."
"All right, then let's skip Christmas this year."
Marion bolted upright. "The kids'll never let us. Face it, we're trapped."
"Oh, no, we're not."

#

"Can't take that," Joe said.
"What?"
"No room."
Stan groaned and dropped his sound system to one side. "This allowed?" he asked dangling his portable Disc Man in his dad's face.
"Where's your bag?"
Stan returned and threw his duffle into the rear of the van.
Joe faced his son. "Is there a problem?"
"No problem."
The problem is I don't know where I'm going for God's sake.

Stan sat in the back seat as far apart from his sister as the territory would allow and checked out her Old Navy tee shirt.
"You gettin' dropped off somewhere?"
"Like the Bahamas."
"Ooh, like a little mambo on the beach, ooh, how nice."
I can't stand those lame Caribbean spots where everyone pretends they are swells — like greasing up for the show-off tan back home. A couple of years ago I went to Freeport on a lame vacation with my parents — the sailboat ride stunk. For the first time I understood Auschwitz — without the showers. They promised lobster fishing and snorkeling. Actually, I was a captive on this fake sailboat — no sails, no lobster dives, and a ten-second dunk in the ocean took care of the snorkeling. I ended up on a beach covered with litter for a cook-out where I got to watch the crew get stinking drunk. I might never have returned alive. Then there was this guy Howard Hughes who owned the hotel we were staying in — Ishnala — whatever. He'd been imprisoned up there on the top floor — same deal as the phony sailboat — a loser.
"Skiing," Stan whispered. "We're going skiing."
"Sure."
Joe turned off the airport road and headed north on I-75.
"Mystery trip. I love it," Joe said.
"That's right, a live mystery trip," his mother said.
"Upper Peninsula?" Stan asked. "Like skiing?"
Finally his father answered, "Not this trip. This is a special Christmas."
Stan rolled his eyes and silently mouthed, *Fuck!* to his sister, then said, "Not a present in this car. Guaranteed!"
"I never knew anyone who got NOTHING for Christ-

mas," Kathy said. "I can just imagine when Debby says like, 'And what did you get for Christmas, Kathy?' Wow — nothing."

"You have a problem with that?" Joe asked.

"Yes," screamed Kathy.

Stan raised his hands, palms upward. "I'm fine."

How could my parents be this stupid? I'm a captive every day of my God-damned lame life, and now I'm supposed to be on vacation — wow — I can't believe this. Kidnapped — for sure. There are laws against this. I can't trust my sister and now my parents for God's sake? I know there are these kids somewhere in the world that get no presents — lame kids with lame parents — I should feel sorry for them — actually I do — they're probably just like this kid in my class who doesn't brush his teeth — poor asswipe — for God's sake — I can't spend Christmas worrying about lame asswipes.

After lunch at McDonald's, they crossed the Mackinac bridge where Lake Huron, Michigan and Superior waters meet in a spectacular expanse. Small patches of open water lapped at frozen stretches. Once they were across the bridge, Route 2 turned inland toward the west. The scenery diminished to solid forest, then towns dwindled to a couple of buildings.

"What's a pasty?" Kathy asked. The sign loomed almost as large as the A frame shack it covered.

"Sounds like a tattoo," Stan said.

"It's a little meat pie," Joe said. "Everyone has to have at least one pasty in a lifetime. If it weren't so late, I'd stop."

Oh, please, Dad, I need a pasty! As if Dad's life depended on a pasty. He's out there — flipped!

A grimy road sign announced the town of Brevort.

Two gas pumps stood like faded sentinels guarding a Café-Lounge that promised Fine Dining and a Happy Hour. Strings of looped Christmas tree lights with several missing bulbs outlined the roof and windows. Beyond the restaurant VACANCY was printed above a red-lit arrow at the roadside pointing to tiny one-room houses that advertised a motel.

Happy Hour? More like Crappy Hour — like who would come to celebrate at this stupid place? It's empty, for God's sake. At least we aren't stopping here.

He'd given up asking where they were going. Looking out the back window, he spotted a few scattered cabins with woodpiles almost as large as the buildings that lined the road.

"Like where's the town?"

"That was it," Joe answered. "Hang on."

Stan poked Kathy to get a rise, but she disappointed him — just looked out her window.

Those cabins with their woodpiles remind me of our hardware store at home where skimpy piles of six logs are stacked in front of the store — pure rip-off. If there is one thing I can't stand, it's a rip-off. Like this lame freshman, Drucker, whose locker is next to mine — keeps saying how outdated my CD player is. Then one day Drucker offers to buy it off me like for nothing — another rip-off.

Finally, about mid-afternoon, Joe pulled up alongside a snow-covered drive, no house in sight. Stan stared at the blanket of white, no ski hill, no lifts, no chalet. Joe opened the back door, and Stan struggled from the car.

"We walk in from here," Joe said, tossing the kids their ski jackets.

"Wait here, I'll check out the beach for you, Kathy," Stan said. "What's wrong — your tongue stuck?"

They trudged down the rutted road through the snow, struggling under the weight of the baggage and groceries.

"There's no running water," Joe said, "heat or electricity."

Suddenly, a small log cabin appeared in a clearing surrounded by woods.

"First, we have to split wood to start a fire," Joe explained, "then you can prime the pump, Stan."

Has Dad just received some message from Mars or something — Hello down there — No running water!

Hello, Dad, this is your son on EARTH. Couldn't we have voted on this? No heat? I wasn't born with fur — or haven't you noticed. Oh, yes, I forgot to tell you, I am NOT nocturnal — like I need HELP to see at NIGHT!

"I don't believe this," Stan hissed under frozen breath. He stopped, snow well above his knees, and stared at the cabin.

There is three feet of snow on the roof alone.

"Little house in the woods!" Kathy squealed.

"Don't act like you like it." Stan dropped his bag just inside the door.

"Thanks, Stan," Kathy snarled stumbling over his baggage, falling against the lead sink that supported a hand pump.

Stan lugged his belongings into the cabin's main room. It was colder inside than out.

A large cobblestone fireplace covered one wall with a few old logs stacked to the side. Opposite the fireplace a rough-hewn wall extended up to a peaked ceiling. Behind a partition, Stan found two bedrooms with barely enough space in each for two small cots and dumped his belongings on one of the cots.

"Where's the bathroom?"

"Outside," his mother answered. "There's a very nice outhouse just a stone's throw from the back door."

"A *nice* outhouse? Mo-ther, come on, in the winter?"

"That's right. Complete with a catalogue. Is that a problem?"

"Whatever."

People do freeze to death, you know. At least we won't have to worry about coming back here again. We won't be alive. It'll be in the headlines — Spring Thaw Leads to Family of Four Frozen in North Woods. I read where some trappers, men who actually lived in the cold north woods, had frozen to death. Some weird storm had moved in, and they were found perfectly preserved in the snow.

"Go help your father cut wood."

Joe was splitting a small pile of wood. "This won't be enough firewood for us. We'll have to find more logs. Here, take this in to the wood stove. Tomorrow I'll show you how to split wood."

Stan grimaced as Joe piled log upon log onto his outstretched arms. "I love you, too, Dad." His arms ached under the load as he trudged to the cabin, yelling at his sister to open the door.

Parts of the world exploit children — I've read about it. Kathy Lee Gifford got in trouble hiring children from third world countries to work in factories that manufactured her products. I'll save that info in case this gets worse.

He returned in slow motion for another load when Joe motioned him to follow.

Kicking snow from fallen tree after fallen tree, Joe finally picked up one end of a Jack Pine. Reluctantly, Stan knelt and lifted the other end. "This way," Joe said and shoved the log along the near side of a tall strong tree and behind the far side of a second one. He pushed hard against the log. Stan pushed from his end, and with each thrust their combined weight snapped off another clean piece of dead wood.

Big deal — a lever — I learned that in eighth-grade science.

They shoved the log forward a couple of feet and gave another hard push. Crack, another piece fell onto the snow. Finally, they ran out of log. "Find another," Joe said. Stan was ready to quit. At length, stacking what they could not carry, they headed back to the cabin.

"Just in time," Marion said. "The cook stove is worried, but the fireplace is desperate."

"I'm freezing," Kathy called from the living room. She'd crisscrossed dry sticks on two broken railroad ties that served as a grate. "This okay, Dad?"

"Perfect," Joe nodded. "Forget the pump, Stan?"

Stan pretended not to hear until Joe asked again. "I thought I'd done my share," Stan said.

"Can't handle the pump?"

Stan found an old pail in the corner and went outside to fill it with snow.

Man, it's cold out here. Like my hands have freezer burn. Twenty-four hours ago life was normal. Now here we are pretending to be Eskimos for God's sake. Last year some lame kid in school, probably Drucker, did a report on Eskimos. They all had TVs for God's sake. Wonder where Drucker went for Christmas. He's always bragging about his grandpa with a condo in Colorado. Drucker's probably snowboarding right this minute. I'll never tell a soul about this, specially Drucker. He'd laugh his stupid ass off.

Placing the pail on the edge of the stove to melt, Stan went in to watch them light the fire. Cold from stones on

the hearth pierced his knees. His hands were still fiery red.
"Didn't you put on gloves?" his mother asked.
"No problem."
I wouldn't be caught dead wearing those God-damned gloves or boots or any of that crap.
Sparks ignited the dried branches, and red flames spurted from the split wood. Stan stared into the fire.
The colors are kinda cool — blue — green — red — orange. Too bad we don't have a fireplace at home. Except for the firewood rip-off at the hardware store. Some friend of Drucker's started a fire in someone's garage once — shithead got caught.
Marion got up to start supper. "Where's my water?"
Stan went back to the kitchen and poured melted snow water on the plunger. He forced the squeaky pump handle up and down, poured more water on the plunger, then pumped up and down and up and down, poured more water, but nothing happened.
"This thing's broke," Stan said stepping aside.
"Can I help?" Kathy hissed moving in front of him.
"Outta my face, idiot."
He dribbled more water into the plunger, trying to pump at the same time. Still no results. Kathy grabbed the pail from him and dumped all the water in the top of the plunger, splashing most of it on the floor. Stan was about to punch her when water began to trickle, dribbles at first, then more rapidly the faster he pumped.
"I did it," Kathy boasted.
"You did not, " Stan said shoving her aside.
They stopped arguing as the sporadic flow of water from Stan's fervent pumping mesmerized them. Kathy cupped her hands and sipped some. "Umm, delicious."
"Here, you pump now," Stan said, cocking his head to

one side, as he leaned forward. "You drink the sissy way," and widened his mouth beneath the spout.

Kathy gave two hard pumps, and water gushed full force in Stan's face splashing all over him.

"You shithead," he snarled, jumping away, shaking his wet hair all over her. "Gosh, look what you've done to my jacket."

"It's just water."

Joe stood in the doorway. "And let there be water."

#

The next afternoon was billed as Christmas-tree shopping day. Stan understood this was Joe's choice of words meant to lessen the culture shock.

It was overcast and dry. Light snow fell intermittently.

I would never go along to choose a God-damned tree if I was home. I'd be hanging out somewhere cool. This will take forever. Like now we have a whole God-damned forest to find the perfect tree. Christmas trees are lame, everyone knows that.

"Here," Joe said to Stan.

"What's this for?"

"It's a hat to protect you from the hunters."

Stan turned the hat around in his hand and passed it back to his dad.

"You have to wear it," Joe said.

Stan stuffed it in his pocket. "What kind of hunters?"

"Deer hunters. It's deer season."

An orange hat, for God's sake! I wouldn't be caught dead wearing this lame monstrosity. Hunters? I thought we were the hunters looking for the tree. Now we've got hunters hunting us. I don't believe this.

They walked single file through the canopied forest. Stan brought up the rear. That way he could drop back, pretend he wasn't with them. He watched little furry creatures dart into crevices and disappear.

No one's following these little guys around, telling them what to do. How come these creatures get to have so much fun? So much freedom — nice. I have to account for everything — to everyone, for God's sake. I heard there was this wolf-boy, like he'd been abandoned by his parents and raised in the wild by wolves. Lucky dawg.

Suddenly, he wanted to tell someone how he'd seen these little furry animals. He called ahead to the others, "I think someone's been here before."

"What do you mean?" his dad shouted back.

"This path — it's been used," Stan yelled.

"Not by people, except for the hunters," Joe said. "It's a deer path. There are lots of paths like this in the woods. It's fun, kind of like being a deer."

They don't get it. Oh yeah, the hunters. Watch out for the hunters!

They stopped often to look at the merits of a particular tree. It had to look good from at least three sides.

Twice Stan stopped with them, getting more and more bored looking at trees. Suddenly, dropping back he thought he saw a flicker in the woods. "Hey, look! There's a deer," he called ahead. Everyone stopped.

"Oh, yeah, sure, Stan," Kathy said.

"I love you, too, Kath."

Several times Stan thought he saw a baby deer, and he yelled at them to look, but it always turned out to be a fallen log or a brown-leaved shrub that matched the deer's winter coat. Finally, they no longer stopped to look when he called to them.

I'll find my own deer!

He dragged behind while Kathy and his parents trudged

from tree to tree.

All of a sudden, Stan spotted movement off to one side. He was positive it was a deer nestled in a thicket. Slowly, he crept toward the form. Something moved slightly. He was right. It was a fawn. Slowly, it rose on slender, gangling legs. Never had he seen anything so cool. A white flash over his shoulder caught his attention, but when he looked back, the baby deer was gone. He raced to tell his family, flying over fallen logs.

"Mom, Dad, Kathy, wait up. I saw a deer, a real deer, a baby," he cried.

"Sure, Stan, sure," Kathy said, "and we saw three, didn't we, Mom?"

"Now, now," Marion said.

"That's nice," Joe said, continuing his search for a tree.

"It doesn't matter if you saw it," he yelled to Kathy, "because I did and you didn't!"

Stan trudged along behind. Finally, they found an almost perfect tree. Joe insisted they all help chop it down and take turns carrying it on their shoulders.

Bang! Bang! The sound of gun shots ricocheted through the trees.

"What's that?" Kathy yelled.

"Deer hunters. Stan, put on your hat!"

Oh my God, they're shooting my deer!

#

Back at the cabin they placed the tree in the exact center of the main room, beneath the peaked ceiling.

"This is the best tree we've ever had," Kathy said.

Stan stood back and looked at the day's production but could not get the young deer out of his mind.

I've never had a pet or anything, but that deer, it's like lying right here. Please let it be alive, not shot by some lame hunter.

On Christmas Eve they strung popcorn and cranberries to decorate the tree. Stan was still obsessed with the small deer in its nest, hidden amongst brown cover, about to escape.

It rises slowly, here one minute, gone the next. Who cares if Kathy believes me. I can see it! Come on, little fella. Fly across the land — over logs, under bushes, disappear in a flash. I won't let them shoot you.

After supper Kathy finished sweeping pine needles from beneath the tree. Marion shivered as the fire died down. She drew a blanket around her shoulders and blew out the candles. A patch of cloud slipped from the face of the moon, allowing white light to pierce the forest canopy and stream into the tiny room. Suddenly, the entire tree was illuminated by moonlight. Little stars appeared wherever moonlight touched the cranberries.

Stan sat cross-legged on the floor.

Kathy held the broom.

"Look," she said, pointing to the reflection on the wall. "Our own Christmas play, and I'm the shepherd."

"Well — I'll be —," Joe said.

They drew closer to Stan.

"Hey, Mom, pull that blanket up on your head like you're Mary," Kathy said.

Stan looked up at his family and back to their silhouetted scene on the wall. *I wish we had a deer for the camel.*

IN SIGHT

My grandmother had lived to be very old. I don't miss her but I wish I could feel something, some kind of emotion, as I stare at this mish-mash collection. There is no order or sense of direction to it — like a love of spoons or even of brass bells.

Disturbed dust particles cloud the swath of sunshine that cuts through the room. The lighted pathway ends abruptly where shelves cover one wall of an alcove. Dust has been allowed to gather on trifles that line the shelves. Carefully I wrap each item in newspaper and place it in a cardboard box beside me. Poofs of dust animate the bright stream every time I remove another treasure. My mother is in the other room doing the same thing. We are helping my grandmother move from off this earth. Everything smells old.

"Take what you want for your apartment," my mother calls to me. But this is just an assortment of cheap odds and ends. I push my grandmother's rocker aside. The shove sets it in motion. Back and forth it rocks as though someone were in it. I've hardly been here to visit since Grandmother moved to Florida, but neither has my mother.

I try to imagine Grandmother in this corner, rocking away, listening to the radio, reminiscing or reading her mail — she loved to get mail. I feel guilty for never writing. I'd thought about it, but somehow never did, except to thank her for some birthday present that I knew my mother had bought anyway. By the same token, I know my mother signed my name to birthday and Christmas gifts for Grandmother. I wonder if any of those found their way into this alcove.

Long ago I decided I hated "things" sitting around. I like a bare look. Clutter depresses me, so convinced am I that possessions possess one.

The chair continues to rock, somehow perpetuating its own motion, confined within the sun's brilliance. Grandmother's brother had built the rocking chair. It must be perfectly balanced. It reminds me of one of those wooden birds stuck on the side of a bowl that once set in motion pops its head up and down incessantly, pretending to drink water. These are the kinds of things I remove and wrap, dime-store variety. A painted pottery milkmaid with an opening on top probably held fresh flowers at one time. It's the cheap kind of vase florists send. Next to it lives a little clay pinch-pot filled with rubber bands. How long have they been forced companions? The only book is a dictionary. At one time Grandmother did crossword puzzles.

Why would anyone keep all this junk? I want to throw it all out, but my mother is adamant about packing everything. Like mother, like daughter. Well, thank God I'm different. Thank goodness my shelves are filled with books. Is this how we all end up? So what if people *had* given Grandmother all these tacky mementoes. Am I, too, destined to sit amongst cheap memories in lieu of people?

A patch of sun creeps along behind me as I work my way along the shelves. I sense its warmth gently pushing me along. Mechanically, I pack item after item, none of which means anything to me. The rocker has slowed to a stop, its creaking silenced, now out of the sun's reach. I lean over and with a light touch start it rocking again. I like hearing it squeak against the carpet.

"There you go, Grandmother," I smile at my foolishness. By squinting I can see her sitting there in a cotton dress and sensible shoes. I want to picture my grandmother wearing a printed house dress rather than one of those polyester pant suits.

I reach for the next item patiently waiting to be wrapped into oblivion. A plain brown pot on the top shelf looks vaguely familiar and stops me. The jar has a pebbly stone finish. A small chip mars the rim of its lid. On top sits a crude-looking honey bee, one wing broken off, the other chipped at its tip. Slowly I rotate the jar. "Honey" is etched on the opposite side where yellow paint still heightens some of the letters.

Suddenly a little girl emerged onto a sunny sidewalk, scurrying along toward a garage sale. It was early summer, light and airy. Card tables displaying myriads of objects filled a driveway in front of a house at the end of the block. She spotted the honey jar at once. No matter that the bee's wings were broken. It was marked 25 cents, her whole allowance.

I try to recall giving it to her, but all I can remember is buying it. She kept it all those years — it must have meant a lot. I shudder at the effect of dismantling my grandmother's life, penetrating into some deep unknown layer up to now kept private. An impulse urges me to put everything back in its place.

For a long moment I sit on the floor immobilized, holding the honey jar, watching the slackening pace of the rocking chair. Rhythmically, I tap the rocker with my toe. I think about where I might put the honey jar.

I jump when my mother suddenly appears at my side.

"What a mess," she moans and plops down in the rocking chair. "I suppose I'll end up keeping most of it." Leaning back and closing her eyes, she begins to rock. "Did you find anything you wanted to save?" she asks.

I stare at the rocker, at its abrupt transformation into the next generation and turn away from its frightening effect.

"No, I don't think so."

ERNIE'S GONE

Ernie's gone. The bass we caught together last night swims in the live box alongside the pier. I can't bear to clean it yet. Tonight I went fishing alone, but it wasn't the same. I was anxious about getting back to the cabin. Before Ernie left this morning he asked when I would be in the cabin tonight. He figured I'd be fishing. I said by 8:30, and he promised to call by then.

Last night after we caught our bass, not a bad one — a two-pound smallmouth that took a considerable amount of time to net — we lingered to watch the sunset. An eagle had cruised by moments before. The water had a slight ripple from an offshore breeze. Ernie decided to switch from his plastic, very smelly, worm to a live one, and he baited it himself.

"I didn't know you could hook on a worm."

"No problem," he said.

"How come you don't put minnows on your hook, then?"

Ernie laughed. "You never showed me."

A deer appeared on the shoreline. "It's a girl," he told me.

Ernie and I talk sparingly in the boat.

"Whoosh," he says when he gets a strike. Ernie knows a strike from a weed. Ernie knows a lot of things. He knows I like to go fishing. Sometimes we talk about baseball or one of his friends. In the past he's said, "Isn't it nice to be alone?" or "Isn't it nice to get away from the cabin?"

He had an accident in his bed the first night he arrived. After we changed the bed, and still groggy from being awakened from a sound sleep, I asked him if this ever happened twice in one night. "It's very rare," he said confidently and immediately fell back to sleep.

A couple of years ago while we were fishing, a loon introduced him to echoes. Ernie never knew about echoes. We were fishing in a bay at the south end of the lake. A loon flew overhead trilling its flute-like tremolo. Its call reverberated against the bluff on shore. The loon repeated its song several times. Echoes rang out one over another until it sounded like a multitude of chimes. Spellbound, Ernie forgot about fishing. When the loon had flown past, Ernie began his own tremolo that echoed repeatedly. I was spellbound. It was equally beautiful, and I told him so.

I used to worry that once he returned home, Ernie would forget about our fishing forays or river trips down the St. Croix like the time we had to build a makeshift fireplace in the ground, when he burned his mouth on a red hot marshmallow, and we had to douse him in the river. I'm not so concerned now that he's visited again this year. He remembers all right. He wanted to fish and canoe. He wanted to build fires and face red-hot marshmallows. We sat together for thirty minutes in the sand driveway trying to start a fire by twirling a stick in a hole we drilled in a pine board. He saw his first bear this year, took it right in stride, not too excited, not too blasé.

We played a card game by the fireplace after dark, and he laughed hysterically saying, "I didn't know you were so funny, Grammy, you should go on Saturday Night Live." But Saturday Night Live is far away from Gordon. We have no television, just loons, herons, birds and animals for sound effects and luckily, Ernie. We have just a Sunfish to sail, no Wave Runner for excitement, although he does threaten to buy me one for Christmas.

I don't expect Ernie to remember he promised to call. He's only six. Besides the phone company's been working on the lines, and I doubt if he could get through.

But surprisingly at 8:35, five minutes past his bedtime, the phone rings. I can hardly hear him through the loud hum on the line. I think he tells me about a friend who found a fish in the street. I say I miss him. He asks me if I caught a fish tonight. I say no, but I love him, and we hang up.

I build a fire and look over at the difficult grown-up jigsaw puzzle for which he found a couple of pieces yesterday.

I don't know, I think I have to let that bass in the live box go so we can catch it again next year — no problem.

SONG OF URSULA

Ursula stands behind the podium. Judge Cohn introduces her as a newly naturalized citizen — was it only last year? She hears only snatches. "From Eastern Germany — fled the Russians in 1945 — father a prisoner of war for six years." He neglects to mention her father was in the Nazi army. "Moved to Detroit in 1972, married a native Detroiter." No mention her husband is Jewish. She tunes out the embarrassing parts, the unwarranted praise, so unnecessary hearing it retold.

She confronts the color spectrum of faces, few as white as hers. "...her life was in chaos...," Judge Cohn is saying.

This morning's phone call intrudes — her sister from Germany wanting to know what would she say. The war? No, no — not the war, her sister warns — everyone lived that story. Family doesn't talk about it — put the past behind you.

The American flag tops her height yet droops at her side. It's supposed to billow. This is America. I'm a citizen now. I must make them believe. She dreads not ringing true.

Seated before her are those who have already been

sworn in, all citizens now, no longer petitioners for naturalization. They've pledged their allegiance. Everyone's name and place of birth has been announced. "We're well represented throughout the world," the immigrations officer said of them.

"Thank you so much for asking me to speak to you — new citizens," she begins, her voice sounding strange to her. "It is a privilege."

Shoulder to shoulder with the American flag, she'd never felt it so close before. "Almost a year ago I sat where you are sitting now, stood in your shoes, and took the same oath to become a United States citizen." She glances down at her notes. "It was not a decision for me as it often is for those immigrants who are forced to leave their native country because of religious or political persecution." She hesitates. This is not sounding right.

Suddenly it's Spring, 1945. She turns away from her speech and begins again, "The war was just ending, the bombing horrendous. Our city was in flames. Incredible! Who was bombing, anyway? The Russians, the Germans, the Americans, the British? I can't remember. People burst in on us to take shelter. For days we'd been living in a basement beneath the harsh sounds of steel-plated shoes resounding through concrete walls, rhythmic, determined, disciplined steps pounding the pavement just outside slits of glass window at street level. Suddenly — where was the bombing? It had stopped. A strange new silence, the silent sound of thick rubber-soled shoes beneath khaki pant legs. American soldiers quietly pulled rolls of wire along the concrete. I pressed my face against the pane — my first look at Americans, no faces, just khaki pants and silent rubber-soled shoes passing on the walk above, a hiatus from all the explosion.

"How could such a strange, horrible interlude have interrupted the midst of our normalcy? What am I saying to you? I saw civilized people become animals. All laws of human decency were suspended. War — it's unbelievable, but it's true."

Her thoughts race on.

"We all knew that when the war ended, if the Russians were coming, we must flee to the western part of Germany where the Americans were, where my grandmother lived. My mother understood life would be safe within the American sector. When we abandoned our house, our lovely house, I remember such strange smiles on the neighbors' faces. They were plotting to loot our house as soon as we left.

"There was only one route. Four of us, my mother, my aunt, my sister and I set out to walk the fifty miles to where we heard there was a train that would take us across the border, to Western Germany, to safety we'd been told. I was nine, my sister seven. I had my teddy bear and an extra pair of shoes in a little back pack, all Mother would allow me to carry. Mother said, 'if we get separated, we will meet in Frankfurt.'

"I heard wild explosions as nearby bridges were blown up. Files of people walked along the road pulling their belongings in carts. Along the way, we asked for shelter in barns. Sometimes farmers gave us something to eat, sometimes not. If not, we had to steal — a potato, an apple, whatever we could find. One night we were hiding in a root cellar with a hundred others when the Russians came looking for Germans. No one coughed or hardly breathed. Miraculously we escaped undetected.

"Our feet blistered and near exhaustion, we reached the refugee-filled train station where we would flee to the west.

Hundreds shoved, to the left, to the right, all trying to climb aboard at the same time. It was a coal train. I lost sight of my mother. My sister and I were pushed up the train steps by the crowd, separated from my mother and aunt. They didn't make it on board. Suddenly there we were all alone, seven and nine years old, tucked in a niche on a coal train, three hundred miles from Frankfurt. When the train reached the border, they wouldn't let anybody across, not even trains. My sister and I lived in a refugee camp with many other people. In vain, we searched faces, recognized no one. For weeks we went everyday to the station master to ask when a train was leaving.

"One day a train with wounded soldiers came from the east that was scheduled to cross the border to Western Germany. The station master hid us between the wounded in a compartment. With tears streaming down my cheeks, I listened to the hollow rattle of the train passing over the trestle as we crossed the Russian/American border into Western Germany. We were free! But the train stopped just inside the border.

"Now we were told we must find a train to Frankfurt, but there was none. Thousands of refugees swarmed about in search of trains — to anywhere. There were no schedules and no one to ask. We were so hungry.

"I heard someone say, 'Why don't you go over to that American troop train?' It was parked on a sidetrack and was rumored to have soldiers with food rations.

"I knocked on the side of the box car. Slowly it opened. The whites of eyes in black faces peered out — black arms stretched toward us. I'd never seen a black person before. We stood immobilized — so scared — ready to run — faint from hunger, lost from our mother. The soldiers reached out and gave us their rations, tins of food —

so colorfully packaged. We loved that. Time after time we returned to those black soldiers. Again and again they shared their food with us. They saved our lives. I'd give anything if I could find those men today.

"One day, on one of our trips to our American saviors, a man that my mother had sent to search for us somehow spotted us amongst the teeming crowd on the station platform and showed us her picture. We trusted him, and he took us to our mother. So the story had a happy ending."

Suddenly, an open patch in the sky highlights a family with two little girls in the middle of the room. She speaks directly to the two girls, cannot turn away from them, "Yes, luckily we were saved. And so are you."

This morning's drive downtown creeps into her thoughts, her frustration mounting with news reports, ashamed of her hypocrisy.

"Today's news keeps us well informed of the bad, less often the good, and recently I realized that I, too, had fallen into bad thoughts, condemning along with the rest. Only yesterday I heard myself criticize the President, the Governor, the United States government, this stupid election, African-Americans, whatever. My memory is short.

"I stand before you in this predominantly African-American city of Detroit, admitting that I locked my car doors on my way here this morning. Hello! Wasn't it those same African-Americans that saved these two little girls?"

Suddenly she realizes she hasn't said a word from her speech and begins to read:

"I stand before you shoulder to shoulder with the American flag and — yes, unafraid to admit the United States' weaknesses along with my own, but so proud to be a citizen and living in this city and country."

She stops — insincere — too practiced. Quickly she scans the last lines of her speech:

Compared to the rest of the world, democracy works. At times messy and confusing, democracy still is the best form of government known to mankind. About the English language, I say 'learn it thoroughly.' Learn five new words every day. Pronounce your TH's and R's. Nowhere have I experienced such openness, such friendliness. Most cultures seal themselves off. Forty-two million immigrants have settled in this country, a population shift unequaled on this planet. Be serious about your citizenship. Defend your newfound freedom.

The audience stirs, and she looks up, pushing aside her notes.

"Soon after the war, I saw Americans driving cars that were brilliantly colored. Somehow it all fit in with the African-American soldiers' smiles, their tins of meat so appealingly packaged, bright red and yellow candy wrappers, glossy papers — so enticing amidst the drab, dusty greyness I'd known. They fed more than my hungry stomach, they fed me hope."

She steps back from the microphone. The National Anthem begins as Judge Cohn steps alongside her. She looks out on faces that are her face, eyes that are her own.

She's found her voice.

FAREWELL

Susan chose to sit near the front of the company jet, in one of the four comfortable seats. She watched a group clustered about the foot of the steps leading into the small airplane. A pretty woman carrying a small baby seemed anxious to board the plane followed by another young girl. Behind her stood a tall, thin young man wearing dark glasses, his black hair and moustache in sharp contrast to his pale, emaciated look.

Unable to stand still, the group reminded Susan of cattle about to break and scatter at the slightest provocation. Gusts of cold wind blew hair and coattails about as they turned backs to the frigid air, trying not to lose sight of one another. Fixed smiles perhaps concealed hidden anxieties. No one seemed ready to leave except the tall, sunken-cheeked man, anxious to herd his wife and baby onto the plane, end the farewells.

Those who had come to say good-bye moved closer together, crowding the thin man like a horde of mosquitoes moving in to feed. Awkwardly, he leaned forward to acknowledge a grey-haired woman's cheek, hands briefly holding one another. Squeezed beneath his arm was a packet of large manila envelopes.

Susan stared at the privacy she was invading. An older man wearing dark glasses was the last to approach and clasped the young man's hand and arm pulling him closer just a moment too long, longer than a casual good-bye. Visibly shaken, the gaunt young man turned his back and guided his wife and baby onto the aircraft.

Susan rose to relinquish her seat for the mother and baby and moved to sit on the small narrow seat stretching across the rear of the plane. The tall thin man and the young girl, who Susan now learned was his sister, sat on either side of her.

"Wouldn't you like to sit together in the middle?" Susan asked the man. "You'll have more room for your legs." She looked at his long legs jammed against the seat in front.

"No, thanks," he answered, his raspy voice retreating into his sunken chest.

The plane's engines roared. Susan settled back until they were aloft. The young mother retrieved a bottle from her carry-on bag and fed her baby. A frightened look captured her eyes. One free hand grasped the armrest so tightly that her knuckles turned red, then white. Glancing worriedly at her husband and sister, she grimaced, then forced a toothy smile.

Susan smiled reassuringly, hoping to allay the young mother's fear as the small craft bounced about climbing through broken clouds.

X-RAYS — DO NOT BEND — was stamped across the top of the envelope the thin man held on his lap. He did not seem at all frightened by the rough flight. Susan marveled at how relaxed he seemed except for his labored breathing. Once aloft, as the flight smoothed out, the beautiful baby fell asleep in his mother's arms, eyelids barely fluttering, yielding to a quieter world.

"You have a beautiful baby. How old is he?" Susan asked the man.

"Four months, they say he's big for that. Excuse my voice," he said trying to clear his throat. "It's from a tube that was down my throat. I just got out of the hospital — had a gall bladder operation."

"Your x-rays — you're taking them to Florida?"

The man looked down. "I don't want to depress you."

"No, please tell me."

"They found I have inoperable cancer in my pancreas, liver and colon. Actually I'm on my way to Freeport to a clinic in the Bahamas for special treatment. It has to do with immunology and blood. Have you heard of it?"

"No."

"They told me here in Detroit I should have chemotherapy — I wanted to try this method first."

"Don't worry about depressing me. By the way, I'm Susan Sherwood."

"Nice to meet you, Susan, Henry Wilcox. I guess your husband is the boss."

"Not quite. We're going to a conference in Freeport."

"That's my wife, Donna," he said gesturing toward his wife and baby. "The baby is Tim."

Susan shifted her position, not sure how to begin. "Believe it or not, Henry, three years ago I was told I had lung cancer. I was convinced that meant a year or two at most for me. They operated and removed my lung, but it wasn't cancer. I couldn't believe it — they'd been so sure. It turned out to be a fungus."

Henry looked over his glasses and said, "Hmm."

Susan was sorry she'd mentioned her good fortune but

continued, "My thinking has changed a lot since then."

She watched Henry's baby cuddled in his wife's arms. "Henry, I want to tell you about a story I've just written telling what I went through. I hope you don't think I am forward. I have the story with me. I needed to put the whole thing on paper."

Henry stared at his wife and baby. Susan guessed he wasn't interested in her experience.

"I have the story with me. Would you like to read it?"

"I would," Henry said.

Susan rummaged through her tote bag and produced her eight-thousand word story about the worst trauma of her life. She handed it to him. "We can talk when you finish — if you want." She felt foolish thrusting her innermost thoughts upon him.

While Henry read Susan concentrated on baby Tim's mother. What a healthy, good-looking woman. Now that the flight was smooth she looked as though she hadn't a care in the world. She smiled at the baby cradled in her arms. He wakened and looked up at his mother as though her love had penetrated his sleep, injecting him with the strength to reenter the world. The baby looked even more beautiful than before. Where his skin had looked soft, it now was lustrous and glowing pink, every muscle vibrant as he squirmed within her embrace. Now he scowled, and a demanding cry sent his mother rummaging though her tote bag for a bottle of milk. Susan held back smarting tears, overwhelmed with the rush of vitality.

Suddenly, Henry's presence overpowered her, and she was ashamed to admit she felt cancer sitting beside her, repulsed by his sickness, wanting desperately to change places with the mother. If only she could hold the baby, feel life.

Finally, Henry turned the last page of her manuscript and stared into space.

"Did it depress you?"

"No, no, not at all. Actually, I've had these feelings but haven't said them. May I keep the story?"

"Yes, of course. I have other copies."

"I'd like Donna to read it."

A shiver crept through Susan. To think her story had meant something to him — more than just venting her own anguish. How then can I sit here, she thought, afraid of a man with cancer, seeing only the disease, not seeing the man.

Henry turned back through the pages of the story. "I liked this part," he said, "where the person with cancer tries to tell her tennis friend, but the friend won't talk about it." He paused, took off his glasses and wiped his face and eyes with his handkerchief. "One of my friends called the other day. He happens to be a doctor, which really gets me because he has to deal with this kind of stuff all the time. Anyway, I think he expected Donna to answer the phone, and when I answered, he sounded surprised. He never asked how I felt or talked about anything normal but just said he was very sorry about the bad news. I don't need anyone to feel sorry for me. He said he knew I was a strong guy and to keep up a stiff upper lip. Suddenly, I wasn't anyone he knew anymore. I'd become a victim — like all the rest he'd known, doomed. I wanted to ask him what he thought about the hockey play-offs — we'd gone to the season games together — but he couldn't hang up fast enough."

He's waiting for me to say something, Susan thought.

Finally she said, "He hurt your feelings."

"Damn right it hurt — like the real me was invisible —

or maybe already dead."

"Something else I discovered when I thought I had cancer — "

"What's that?" Henry asked.

"It's that it wasn't all that bad."

"What do you mean?"

"The thought of dying. It didn't seem so bad. Do I sound strange?"

Henry straightened in his seat, assuming a new energy. "I know what you mean," he said quickly. "That's how I feel sometimes, but it sounds so funny to say it. I didn't know anyone else felt that way. You're the first person I've talked to about dying."

"It would be good to talk to someone else with cancer, Henry. It might help your family, too. Maybe you'll get to know some other people at the clinic in the Bahamas."

Henry was looking back through the story again.

"There's something else you say in here. It reminds me of my dad. Did you see the man in the dark glasses who came to see us off? He had on those glasses because he cries when he thinks about me. Just like the girl in the story who said, 'I can't stand to watch them watch me.' I feel sorrier for my dad and her" — he nodded toward his wife who was playing with the baby — "much more than for myself."

"Do you get tired, Henry?"

"I sleep a lot. I've lost thirty pounds. I try to eat, but I'm not hungry."

"Let your dad cry in front of you. He'd feel bad if you thought he didn't care."

"I hadn't thought about that."

They were distracted by loud cries from the baby. Donna's sister produced a diaper and plastic bag, and once changed the baby quieted.

Before Susan's eyes the baby grew into a rowdy boy kicking a soccer ball down a sidewalk, moving from side to side to keep the ball on a straight path. He cried out and laughed, tossing his hair in exhilaration, his face to the sky.

Henry coughed, and Susan noticed how frail he looked. Once again she felt herself withdraw from his illness.

"How long will you stay in the Bahamas?"

"The first two weeks will be tests, and if they decide to treat me, it will be another six weeks. I can always go home and have chemotherapy. I doubt if any of it will make a difference."

"It's worth a try, though."

"At least this treatment doesn't make me sick."

"Have you ever been to the Bahamas, Henry?"

"No."

"Do yourself and Donna a favor, Henry. Walk the beach, swim in the sea — it's like an emerald — hold Donna in your arms and watch the sun set over the water — feel the romance. Walk beside her, Henry. Do it every day."

Henry nodded.

"Write down your thoughts, for her, and him." She nodded toward his wife and son and then wrote her address on the manuscript.

It was hot on the plane now as they descended, and the baby began to fuss. Donna and her sister were clearly excited to be landing and could not contain their smiles.

Rental cars pulled alongside the aircraft as they left the plane. Henry stood close to Susan as they watched the luggage being unloaded and reloaded into respective trunks.

Henry leaned down to Susan, for now he stood much taller than she. "I must thank you," he said.

"For what?"

"You've given me a real lift."

Susan squeezed his hand. He moved even closer, his mouth to her ear and whispered, "I'll write you my last thoughts."

Henry drove off with his family toward town. The phrase *island paradise* would never sound the same again as Susan pictured exotic dancing, piña coladas, Henry, and a cancer clinic.

RUNNING

Fresh air expanded her lungs. Concentrating on the sensation, she sucked in all the air she could hold before pressure forced her to push it out. A purification process.

Karen quickened her pace as she rounded the stone boulder that marked the beginning of her Monday morning run on the golf course before anyone teed off. For the next hour she would let her body and mind go, escape, allow each muscle to do its job. She came here to feel wild.

Bill and the kids were still asleep. This was *her* time before succumbing to a routine frustratingly fragmented into twenty-minute episodes. Only she knew how it gnawed at her. What exactly *did* she accomplish in those twenty-minute segments? She knew to the second how long it took to finish each chore before chauffeuring the kids. Would she be remembered for how many beds she could change or the number of laundry loads between picking up her son from swimming practice and delivering her daughter to ballet? Would that promise her immortality?

She took another deep breath and relished being alone. Seldom did she feel so unique as when running in this paradise. Occasionally, loneliness crept into her euphoria, just a momentary anxiety, but she shook it off, blocked out the nagging uneasiness, returned to her state of wholeness, no cracks.

Linden leaves trembled in the slight breeze, provocatively flashing silvery white from their undersides. Flirting goldfinches flitted busily about while others swooped upon insects. From nearby underbrush she recognized a pheasant's cacophonous mating call. June took the cake for all seasons, so pregnant, so full of intrigue.

Turning south at the golf-course perimeter, she ran along the twelfth fairway. A young man drove a noisy mower along the edge of the rough. Generally, the workmen avoided her. Annoyed at having her reverie disturbed, she glared but couldn't help noticing how muscular the young man was. A thick shock of sun-bleached hair made his smooth, young face seem tanner than it probably was. He grinned and then smiled even more broadly the closer he came.

"You're early," he called.

Puzzled, she looked twice at him, not recognizing his face, not sure she'd heard him correctly over the noise of the mower. She must have misunderstood. Ignoring his overture, she continued her run around the periphery of the golf course onto the front nine.

She found her stride. It was a good run.

She was about to cut across the ninth fairway in front of the green that would bring her to the boulder where she'd entered the golf course when the blond Mower Man reappeared on his machine driving directly toward her, smiling and waving as though he knew her.

He *is* friendly, she thought, mildly flattered by his attention. He must have seen me here before and she returned his wave as she ran past the boulder toward home.

Wednesday morning, when she came again, the air was soft, not too humid, perfect for running. Suddenly, along the twelfth fairway there was the Mower Man, as though magically summoned from a sand bunker. This time, his smile seemed different, as though he found her very attractive. She passed him quickly, deciding not to smile if she encountered him again, not sure why she felt so self-conscious. Who did he think he was anyway?

Back home showering, she stared at her thin nude figure reflected in the mirror. She'd never considered herself beautiful. But at least I'm trim, she told herself, running her hands full length up her body then slowly back down. Her breasts were still firm, her skin smooth and taut. But more than looking good she loved feeling supple, curling up in a corner with Shakespeare, sitting cross-legged with the kids playing a game, or on the floor watching TV with them.

She avoided looking at the wrinkles creasing her neck and face reminding her of the big four zero next year. And now here was this kid in his twenties looking at her in a way her husband hadn't for several years. She had to admit she liked the attention. She pictured newspaper photos of aging female celebrities arm-in-arm with some teen-aged rock star and imagined having a young lover. It would be different.

The next day toward the end of her run, Mr. Mower Man emerged from nowhere. She was headed up the last fairway toward the boulder and out of the club when she saw him. He wore that same grin, more than a casual smile, more like an invitation. This is ridiculous, she thought. Against her better judgment, she smiled back. All the same, she *did* like his finding her attractive, the attention of another man, especially a younger one. It made her feel soft-shouldered, a sensation she'd almost forgotten.

In truth, she had to admit her own marriage was sexually blah. Her husband no longer excited her, nor she him, she assumed. Nor had they discussed it. At least they rarely argued. That was a plus. A silent comfort existed between them, but excitement? Passion was long gone. She'd had hopes for romance during an out-of-town trip they had taken last month, hoping a hotel room might start something. But driving home in the car, she realized that nothing different had happened after all, nothing apart from their usual non-verbal routine. They were more like brother and sister. Their lovemaking seemed almost incestuous, pathetic, amusing her because there was no turning back from it. She took care of him like an older sister. He responded like an appreciative brother.

"Do you have your raincoat?" she'd asked before leaving the hotel room, and of course, he didn't. She'd developed an assertive independence during their marriage, not so much because she'd meant to, but rather like vapor, quiet and unnoticed, she'd filled a void.

At home that night, Bill let the phone ring several times before answering it. Karen glanced up annoyingly from her book.

"Never mind, they hung up," he said.

Karen picked up the phone when it rang seconds later. "Hello," she said into a dead line.

Almost immediately it rang again. This time Karen said harshly, "Who *is* this?"

The caller responded with rapid, heavy breathing. Disgusted, she hung up. Her mind flashed to the Mower Man.

Anxious to run the next morning, Karen crept from bed and put on her new purple and white jogging suit. She glanced in the hall mirror on the way out. It suited her figure. She felt younger than usual.

The golf course was especially inviting this morning. Manicured grass responded like plush velvet beneath each step. Resisting the urge to lie down and roll in the dew, she stepped up her pace. Though not a golfer, she appreciated this atmosphere removed from the rest of the world, perhaps even more than the golfers did.

A pungent smell of freshly cut grass wafted across the fairway, reminding her that the Mower Man must already be on the job. Starting down the next hole, she spotted his mowing machine creeping along, advancing toward her, always toward her. He was looking down at his mower trimming the fairway, and his white blond hair shone in the distance. She hoped he hadn't seen her and cut across the fairway thinking she could avoid an exchange. Noticing was one thing, interaction another. As though anticipating her every move, he swerved across to intercept her path. Her first thought was to run through the woods to another fairway. Instead, she decided to test him. She ran to the other side of the fairway, feeling somewhat foolish as though she were playing fox and geese. He turned his machine to meet her head on. Picking up speed to get out of his range, she saw she would be forced to pass alongside him, and turned left to avoid him. He followed. Now what? His grin was much too big. A look in his eye unnerved her.

"Morning!" he yelled, waving wildly as though he had just won their game. "You look nice today."

She looked the other way without responding. She had not meant to entice him. Suddenly, his attention had taken on an ugliness. Once again, she changed her direction. On cue, he reversed the mower and followed her, laughing loudly. Damn him, she thought. I don't want to deal with this every morning. Can't this jerk leave me alone — just for a few minutes each day? He continued to follow in her path. It was no use to run another direction. She simply could not finish her run. She knew she could outrun his machine, but what if he got off and chased her. Had she encouraged him or was she just imagining all this?

Friday was the last day to run each week because of the weekend golfers. She started out thirty minutes earlier than usual hoping to run alone without the Mower Man. Halfway down the first fairway she caught a glimpse of him through the trees on the front nine. Stay out of sight, she told herself, and disappeared under the tree line.

No such luck, and she groaned as he appeared on the fairway from behind a stand of pine as though he'd been waiting for her. His noisy mower cruised across the fairway near where she was running along the edge of the rough. As he came closer she turned her face from his now familiar leering grin.

"Yoo! Hoo!" he called.

What can I do about this short of not running, she wondered.

Instinctively, she cut across to the opposite rough. He followed in hot pursuit but did not leave his mower. At least he's not trying to grab me, she thought. He probably thinks I'm playing that cat and mouse game again. I'll show him I'm not interested, more frightened than she wanted to admit. She hesitated to look back, but then unable to resist, took a quick peek over her shoulder. He was lunging back and forth over the steering wheel urging his mower on, laughing, slapping his hands up and down on the steering wheel. His white hair flopped forward with each bounce.

Instead of continuing her usual route, she cut through the bushes, around some trees and back out onto the front nine. Now she was truly scared. She no longer trusted his little game or what might happen next and quickened her stride, pushing herself. She had visions of his running after her, chasing her and catching her. A story she'd read about a woman who was attacked and raped while jogging flashed through her mind. That emotional trauma had been well-documented in the article. A lingering fear had left the woman paranoid, unable to run ever again. Panting, Karen raced with all her might toward the boulder at the far end of the club.

Finally out on the street, she was afraid to look back. She imagined him chasing her, now on foot, narrowing the gap between them. She ran like crazy, faster than she knew how until she reached her house at the end of the street. What if he knew where she lived, had watched her? Once inside, she slammed and locked the door, leaning heavily against it, breathless. Running was not worth all this.

As the day wore on, fear of the Mower Man consumed her. Then, slowly anger replaced her fear. Who did this young blond-haired kid think he was anyway, controlling her life this way, ruining her daily salvation?

I'll tell Bill tonight, she thought, but was worried that he would laugh at her, pass it off as a joke, even tease her.

"How silly of you," she could hear him say but then felt a surge of relief as Bill's car turned in the drive.

"Have a nice day?" he asked, tossing his briefcase on the table.

She would have laughed if she weren't so close to crying but said nothing.

The next morning, determined to put an end to this herself, she walked to the maintenance building hidden amidst a wooded area in the center of the golf course. She found the groundskeeper.

"I have a complaint," she began. "I run early each morning," she explained, "here on the golf course before the golfers come out. It means a lot to me, but lately I have been harassed by a maintenance worker. I don't like it." She paused. "He's a young blond worker who mows the fairways each morning. Do you know who I mean?"

The groundskeeper nodded. "I'm sorry about this. I'll look into it," he said.

Karen stood to one side, suddenly miniatured within the huge metal maintenance building. She brushed aside a childlike shyness. "I want you to do more than look into it," she demanded. "I want the man fired. He is harassing me."

The superintendent nodded politely. "Thank you for reporting it."

"Thank you," she said defiantly and finding nothing more to say turned to leave.

A co-worker stood at the superintendent's side.

As she left, Karen overheard the other man say, "You gonna fire the kid? He wouldn't hurt a fly — you know that. Don't fire him, Boss. He wouldn't do any — " His words dissolved in thin air as Karen stepped into the bright morning, pleased with how she'd taken charge.

Once outside she stopped short. What had that worker meant about the Mower Man? "Harmless," he'd said. Even so, she needed to know she was safe.

That night in bed she felt pleasantly exhausted after a busy day with Bill and the kids. Slipping an arm across her husband's chest, she eased her body against him wondering if she should run Monday.

On Monday Karen woke at dawn. She dressed and decided to chance it. Clouds hung on the horizon. It would storm yet this morning, but there was still time to run before it rained. Not a soul was on the golf course as far as Karen could see. Even the birds sounded tentative. She began jogging, slowly at first, scanning the area. No sign of the Mower Man. Slowly she relaxed as she turned onto the next fairway, relieved to be alone. She peered through the pines and bushes, down other fairways. This is heaven, she sighed, savoring her aloneness within her private paradise. It rained hard the rest of the day.

Tuesday was so soggy that Karen had to shorten her run, dodging mirror-like puddles where ducks paddled in small circles devouring loosened morsels. Ironic, she thought, on the days the Mower Man can't run, neither can I.

Finally the rain ended, and Friday produced a fluorescent green carpet, unequaled in Karen's memory. This must have been what Milton meant in *Paradise Lost* when he described Eden after a rainfall. Some of the stanzas lingered in her mind from a long-ago literature class, memorizing the lines not so much as an assignment but from the sheer love of reading them over and over.

On which the sun more glad impressed his beams...
When God hath showered the earth: so lovely seemed
That landscape. And of pure now purer air
Meets his approach...

She smiled recognizing the paradox. Those were Satan's eyes looking at Eden. It reminded her of e. e. cummings' blatant pronouncement: "To Heaven with Hell!" She turned onto the front nine, the last part of her run.

She emptied her mind as was her practice when running

but couldn't keep the Mower Man from invading her privacy. She might never know what happened to him. He'd been gone all week.

The maintenance worker's pleading tone haunted her. "The kid," he'd called him. He was harmless, she'd overheard that much. What if he was slightly retarded? Maybe she'd deprived him of his first job. She imagined him living at home with his parents, riding the bus to work each day, his family so proud of his independence. She remembered his smile, no longer frightening, his child-like grin more understandable now. How sad his look would be when the maintenance boss told him not to return, that he'd lost his job, fired. He wouldn't know why, not understand about being too friendly.

Instead of running straight home, she stopped and sat down on the boulder. Resting her elbow on one raised knee, she sat chin in hand. From here she could see most of the golf course and scanned the lush expanse. A loneliness hung within her, draped her insides. She could put a finger on it but couldn't make it disappear.

Suddenly the drone of a mower sounded in the distance and then emerged, crawling along the edge of the rough. She looked for that white-blond shock of hair. Disappointed, she saw it was someone else, a smaller, dark-haired fellow.

I miss the Mower Man, she admitted and questioned her ability to judge anything correctly anymore.

Last night after dinner Bill had slipped his arms around her from behind, surprising her as she faced the pile of dirty dinner dishes in the sink. He kissed the side of her neck. She passed it off as a routine fraternal peck, suggesting sex, but then when he stepped in front of her and started loading dishes into the dishwasher, something changed. His kiss suddenly meant more to her than pure lust, camaraderie perhaps or a new respect. She couldn't pinpoint it, but it kindled a special warmth inside her.

Stepping aside to make room for him, she'd looked around for another chore so they could continue to work together in the kitchen. She spotted an uneven space between two pictures hanging crooked on the wall. It bothered her, and she moved to straighten them. She used to lose herself within the two scenes of wilderness, one above the other, representing a longed-for world. She'd been drawn to the pictures from the first because of their tranquil aloneness. More and more, though, she only noticed if the pictures were lined up straight — in sync with each other, the ceiling, whatever. She never could get the pictures to stay in line, even after carefully straightening them. They would always appear slightly askew at the next glance. She was destined to straighten them.

On Monday, she came to run as usual. Breathing especially deep, she picked up her pace, resigned to the nagging loneliness she felt here. Oddly, she longed so to be alone, but she couldn't separate the two — the loneliness from being alone. It was a fine line. She tried to block out all thoughts and concentrate on running, on feeling solitary, but worried that the loneliness had magnified to a state of being.

The familiar boulder loomed large at the far end of the fairway. She knew she could not come back again without the Mower Man being here. This was his Paradise where cluttered complexities were hidden from his simple mind.

The sound of a mower interrupted her thoughts. There he was, arm innocently poised to wave. The Mower Man crawled along the fairway riding his machine, his blond hair shining white under the sun.

"Been sick?" she called over the noise of the mower.
"On vacation," he hollered, grinning ear to ear.
She changed course to run alongside him.

OCTOBER LOVE

It's only 8:30 p.m., and you'd think I'd have enough energy to cook for tomorrow's company, but I don't. All I want is to be a frog like Jutta.

So here's a week at the lake with Jutta, the frog.

Did you know you spent much too much time in the hammock today? You tried to read, but the eyes weighed heavily after a few pages, and a short cat nap hit the spot to be interrupted by a fly walking across your cheek. But it was all to the good because now there is food and time to stare into the sky above the cabin through the tallest red pines and their needle fluffs. Clouds across a frameless picture are cast about by the same breeze that rocks your hammock. It looks as though a far away plane is crossing the sky until the dark wings bank, and you recognize an eagle. It heads this way and flies directly overhead, spots you and screeches its treble warning, a silly cry for such a majestic bird. You expect a symphonic call like the loon or wood thrush produce, not such a whining annoyance from our nation's glorious symbol.

Most birds have migrated to bug-infested southlands, and you miss their busyness, their harmonic and cacophonous symphonies. A sole hummingbird remains sounding like a tiny vacuum cleaner, loading up on sugar water from the feeder, freed from unrelenting air attacks by aggressive brethren.

So quiet compared to a month ago, the forest yields a doe, hungry for mushrooms, ambling through the yard with what was her spotted fawn a few weeks ago, now measuring up to her haunch for haunch.

Sunsets are more than ample, often too sweet to bear. You linger each night recording each subtle change in your vocal pallet as it repaints itself — to retrieve some desperate dark night. Each evening grows a touch cooler relinquishing more pungency.

This morning I decide to move the fox that died last night beneath the top step leading to the lake. I haul it into the woods but can still smell it busily decaying whenever the wind shifts or swirls.

There have been no storms, just glorious dry, light-aired days. It's what heaven must be like, if you exist beyond today, when the sun breaks up the woods and creates a new shadow every second. Moving across the sky, it offers you as a sacrifice to the elusive seductive wilderness beyond your hammock.

Here comes a storm. Crashing thunder and lightning neon do battle with the sunset. Trees flatten against each other as winds surge in revolt. You race for cover. All this enhances both the calm and the upheaval, something you cherish.

Yet the fugue, no matter its repetitiveness, comes around as fresh as the loon's prehistoric wail.

Alas, a hopeless captive, you are destined to wallow in the seasons, never content with urban obscenity.

UPSTAIRS

Marf hated cold soup. So each evening she came down early to dinner so they would not arrive to cold soup. Everyone complained about the cold soup, but only Marf had outsmarted them.

A waitress approached her table carrying a large tray of soups. Marf spoke first.

"I'll be dining with Miss Edith and Mr. George tonight," she said somewhat haughtily. In fact, Marf dined every evening with Edith and George, and, in fact, uttered the same words each evening. "Please wait to serve our soup."

"I will not be dining here Christmas Day," Marf added quickly, tilting her well-featured face up in an aristocratic fashion. "I'll be with my family."

The plump, round-faced waitress nodded placidly. "Yes, Ma'am," and then passed on to serve the next table.

It was Christmas week. Marf's table, as did all the tables, displayed an arrangement of plastic evergreens and holly. Marf was used to the real thing but had to concede that the greens did look quite authentic. She touched them anyway, just to satisfy herself that they were artificial.

Marf faced the door to the dining room so she could watch for Edith and George. From habit she smoothed her carefully coiffed hair. For years she had not cut her hair but wore it swooped up and back into a neat French roll. She felt fashionable. Everyone said it was stunning and each week she looked forward to getting her hair done. It made her feel good all over.

She looked at her watch, just as Edith walked in alone.

"Where's George?" Marf asked. Edith's job was to make sure George got to dinner on time while Marf came down to assure they had hot soup.

"Oh, Marf," Edith clasped her hand over her mouth. "I forgot. I had to mail a letter and — " She looked down. "I'll go right up to his apartment and get him."

"It's a room, Edith, not an apartment. We used to live in apartments," Marf reminded her. "You haven't time to go get him. The dining room will be closed by then."

Just then George hobbled through the doorway on his four-legged walker.

"Good evening, ladies," George puffed, "how nice of you to wait for me. Sit down, sit down, Edith."

"I'm sorry, George," Edith said.

"Now, now, you girls fuss over me much too much. I'm here, aren't I?"

Marf tried not to stare at George's palsied hands.

Seated at last, he asked, "Tell me now, what's the news today?"

"Well, let's see," Edith began. "Oh, yes, I'm going to my grand-nephew's for Christmas Day. You remember Russell." Marf tried to remember Russell. Edith continued, "Marf's been invited to her cousin's family for the day, right Marf?"

Marf shifted uneasily in her chair. Actually, she had

not yet received an official invitation, but she was sure her cousin James would call tonight or tomorrow.

"Is that the cousin I met last Easter?" George asked.

"His son's family. They live here in Rockford now," Marf answered, happily avoiding the question.

"Oh, I almost forgot." Edith fumbled in her purse and pulled out a red plastic poinsettia corsage and pinned it on her dress. "Isn't this cute? So Christmasy!" She lifted her lapel to show George. "Didn't you get one, Marf?"

"Yes, but I threw it out. I wouldn't wear one of those things if you paid me," Marf said.

"But those people were so kind to make them for us," Edith said assuming the hurt for whatever volunteer organization had produced them.

"What people? We'll never know even *one* of their names. I think it's downright patronizing."

The waitress came with their bowls of hot soup.

"By the way, Marf," George said. "I think you are ingenious to figure out how we can have hot soup every night."

Marf smiled inwardly. "Thank you, George. Institutions are difficult. I still haven't solved the mashed potatoes and gravy ritual we put up with every other day."

"Don't call Weeping Willows an institution," Edith said. She stopped and snickered behind her napkin. "Do you know what little Russell calls this place?"

"I can just imagine," Marf said.

"Sleeping Widows," Edith giggled, and even Marf had to laugh.

"I'm offended," George interjected, circling his hand shakily about the room. "Just look at all these men."

Marf looked about the brightly lit room of old women seated at round simulated wood-topped tables. There were only two other men, and they sat alone at a table across the way.

"Where?" she asked.

"He's only kidding, Marf," Edith giggled.

"Psst," Marf whispered, "just look at that." She nodded her head toward a little old woman leaving the dining room. "No personal pride, that's all."

"What's the matter with her?" George asked.

"She's wearing those nylon knee-highs again — with a skirt."

"I'll bet she forgot she had them on," Edith sympathized.

"Can't abide it," Marf said with a huff and looked away.

Except for George's describing the extent of the cocaine scare that was on last night's ten o'clock news and small talk here and there, the rest of the meal was eaten in silence.

As they finished dessert, one of the two men across the dining room began shouting.

"There he goes again," Marf said. "Wouldn't you think they'd ask him to lower his voice? Every single night. We're lucky he waited until dessert."

"Poor man," Edith slowly shook her head back and forth.

"Well, if he'd just turn on his hearing aid," Marf said.

"There, you see, the other man at his table reminded him," George said. "Now then," George pushed his chair back and reached for his walker, "will you ladies join me in a stroll?"

"I can just guess where," Marf whispered to Edith.

Once on his feet George led the way out into the hall. He turned to Marf and Edith, "Let's go see what day it is."

Opposite the main desk in the lobby was a large bulletin board that changed regularly showing the day, the month and year. It intrigued Marf how George could make this daily ritual seem so very important. So, each evening, she followed him to the lobby, mainly because she hoped to discover if he really was serious about it or if he simply wanted to make good use of whatever the facility had to offer. In any event, she went along with it, and gradually, without understanding why the routine took on an importance to her, too.

Tonight the board said "December 22, 2000." Marf stared at the date.

But December 22nd and the 23rd came and went with no word from her relatives. If her cousins did not call soon, she might consider calling them.

On Christmas Eve night Marf stayed in her room until the last minute before going down to dinner. The phone call was more important to her than hot soup. At last she could wait no longer and left to go eat. Edith was already at their table, obviously upset.

"I can't find George," she blurted out. "He didn't answer his door, and he wasn't in the TV lounge."

"Oh, dear," Marf said. "We'll go check right after dinner."

"I hope George won't miss the concert."

"Some concert," Marf said.

"Well, it IS Handel's *Messiah*," Edith announced.

"On stereo," Marf retorted.

They hurriedly ate their meal while Marf secretly worried about George.

"Are you all set for Christmas Day, Marf?"

"Oh, yes," Marf lied.

"What time are you leaving?"

"I'm not sure, how about you?"

"My folks'll be here about ten," Edith said.

After dinner the two women walked directly to the main desk.

"Excuse me." Edith leaned over the counter. "Mr. Winston didn't answer his door, Mr. George Winston. Did you see him go out?"

Expressionless, the desk clerk picked up a clipboard and read down the sheet.

Without looking up she said, "Mr. Winston's been admitted to the health-care facility."

"Oh, Marf," Edith gasped. "George has gone *upstairs*! How dreadful! And right before Christmas!"

"He hasn't looked well of late," Marf said softly. She turned her face toward the bulletin board, lest Edith see her emotion. "December 24, 2000," printed in bold red lettering, jumped out at her and then blurred as tears filled her eyes.

The idea of never having to leave Weeping Willows in the event she became ill, that she would always be cared for, had seemed such a comfort to her before moving in. But lately the mere mention of *upstairs* frightened her. It was always there, lurking above her, but suddenly with George up there, it was a *reality*. She was not sure when the idea of upstairs changed from being a comfort to a threat. She tried to pinpoint it. Intellectually and financially it was sound, but now she wondered what on earth had made her want it.

Residents began filing into the chapel for the Christmas Eve concert when Edith spotted their friend Florence across the lobby. Dressed in her winter coat and hat, Florence sat in one of the matching flowered love seats. Facing the door, she leaned forward over an arm-rest worn thin and colorless from others before her who waited in that same anxious position for a ride or a visitor. Edith pulled Marf aside and walked her toward Florence.

"You'll miss the concert, Florence," Edith called.

Without taking her eyes off the double doors that led outside, Florence explained she was waiting for her son-in-law. "He'll be here any minute."

Marf felt a pang at always waiting to be picked up.

"Did you hear about George?" Edith asked.

"George?" Florence repeated vaguely.

"You know, George Winston — he's gone — *upstairs*."

Florence turned from her vigil, her hand pressed against her chest. "Oh, no," she said in what sounded to Marf like a mixture of sympathy and fear.

Just then a young man entered through the double doors, scanning the crowd. Florence rose to join her son-in-law, waving to him, "Here I am — here I am — all ready." He offered her his arm. Florence stopped momentarily at the door and turned to the two women watching her. "Bye," she said smiling and waving, "Merry Christmas!"

Edith and Marf feebly waved to her.

"Well," Edith sighed, "we'd better get on," and they joined the others entering the chapel. They sat stiffly in the church pew waiting for the music to start.

Marf leaned closer to Edith and whispered, "It's too late tonight, Edith, but don't worry, we'll call on George when we get back tomorrow."

By ten o'clock Christmas morning, the phone still had not rung, and Marf began to give up hope. She poured herself another cup of coffee, careful not to spill on the red dress she'd saved for today. Impatiently, she picked up the newspaper. It was very thin. Apparently not much happened on Christmas Day, certainly not in her world.

She looked over at the basket of colorful presents she had carefully wrapped for her relatives. They were presents anyone would like because she'd not been exactly sure who would be there. It was difficult to find presents with a broad appeal, but she'd been pleased with her choices. She felt very apart from the world at this moment with no one to open her gifts.

She rose and circled her room when she remembered George, alone upstairs. Poor George, she thought. Quickly, she gathered her presents and was out the door.

Walking down the corridor, she thought she heard her phone ring but resisted going back — no matter — and continued toward the elevator at the back of the building.

As the elevator door closed, Marf caught sight of Edith coming around the corner, arms laden with presents. She pushed the Health Care button before Edith could see her. Marf had not been *upstairs* since her initial tour of the facility. She hurried out and down the hall, hearing her heels resound against the hard floor. Suddenly she stopped.

"Now why on earth was Edith coming up here?" Marf said aloud. "She should have left by now."

Slowly, Marf walked back toward the elevator. The door slid open, and the two women stood face to face. Edith's chin dropped. "Marf, I thought— ."

"Merry Christmas, Edith."

ATLAS CEDAR

The sole reason I am here is to meet my namesake. It's my mother's fault. My mother and father lived here when I was born. I don't remember it. Do you think a person's name determines their life? If you live in Wisconsin, it does. That's why I'm here. I have to see to believe. I cannot tell you what I've had to surmount because of my name. I wish my mother were alive so I could CONFRONT her. I don't think my father was involved, in the naming that is, but how would I know. While I was still in tenth grade both of them died in a weird car accident near Madison, Wisconsin — Sun Prairie, that's where I grew up.

Who would believe that two sane people from Sun Prairie, Wisconsin, met, married, conceived a child in NEW YORK CITY, then immediately left and took off to return to Sun Prairie, Wisconsin. Unbelievable! It wouldn't be so bad if they hadn't tattooed this impossible name on my future. What were they thinking? I've had to defend it at every corner. First in kindergarten, then grade by grade. One would think unusual names would be standard by the time I graduated from high school and everyone else would be naming their kid something off the wall. No way! Sun Prairie's wallpapered with Pauls, Mikes, Johns, Seans, Toms, and even Zacharys. I could have laughed myself sick over Zachary but for my own name.

That's why I'm headed for Central Park. I've read a bit about Central Park and Frederick Law Olmstead. But I can't blame him either. I don't know though, maybe I should since I don't know the actual birth date of my namesake. Olmstead may have been responsible, providing the seed. I can't afford to stay nearby Central Park so now I'm on the subway into Manhattan. Mom had a distant relative I contacted in New Jersey, and that's where I'm staying.

They were quite surprised when I called, but receptive, sort of. I arrived late yesterday. New Jersey is a little like Wisconsin, hilly but much more crowded. As relatives, they hadn't been close with my folks. In fact, they didn't even know Mom had died in the car accident. I found their phone number in her address book. I couldn't even say they were sad when they heard about Mom.

They didn't seem to know there was a me. But that was a relief because I didn't have to say my name, just my connection as a relative. Apparently, it was enough to know they had some relatives off in the Midwest, west of the Hudson, that they hadn't remembered. It was like finding a new star in the universe, and now they could name it. Sounds fine to me. I'd be happy to be renamed, but for now I'm Margaret's boy.

Over the years, I've looked up a lot of names that sounded strange, especially in the encyclopedia. I've never read about or heard one that's worse than mine. Women seem to have the awfulest names in history like Humility and Contrition. Don't parents understand? They could ruin a kid's life — just with a name like that. I'd never do that to a kid of mine.

Luckily, my namesake won't be upset at meeting me. Not only does he not know I am arriving to confront him, but he could never imagine someone being named after him. I say "him" because I am male so I assume my namesake is male also.

I hop off the subway at 59th Street and head west to the south end of Central Park. It's the end of April. Central Park is dressed to kill. In Wisconsin, the dregs of April haven't decided to yield to Spring let along do battle with Summer. Winter is headstrong in Wisconsin. Here it's in full swing. I wasn't prepared for the daffodil stuff let alone a bird migration. We love the return of songbirds to Wisconsin, but how was I to know they go by way of Central Park. I latch onto a bird-watching tour that leads me through the south end of the park over bridges, wilderness paths, past ponds, streams and swamps. I keep my distance in case the guide would ask why I was hanging around. I'm used to not belonging, so that doesn't bother me a whit. One thing catches my attention, though, the strange names attached to these beautiful birds like Yellow Rumped and Rufous Headed — not all that complimentary.

My cousins asked right off what business I was in. I had to lie knowing I'd disappoint them if I said I'd been fired from McDonald's. That was all right with me, though, because it was a dumb job, and besides, I'd earned enough to achieve my goal. My mom always said I had to set goals. It isn't like she's dead at all. She still keeps telling me stuff like "You don't eat right" and "Set a goal." Well, now my goal is to meet my namesake. I hate him so much. Maybe I can spit on him or turn my back, be rude, throw a dart. Actually, I stuck a couple of darts in my backpack, never know.

There are a lot of dogs in Central Park, almost as many dogs as people. I listen as their owners call them names like Sport, Henry, George. Why do they get decent people names? Dog owners know about lineage. That's how they sell dogs. It's as though my whole lineage was disrupted. My dad's name was Joseph. What's wrong with Joseph?

I head for the Reservoir. There is no straight path in Central Park. It's one continual curve, and I have to trust my instincts. I keep asking passersby, "Where is the Reservoir?" I pass three ponds, one quite large, but obviously it is not the Reservoir. Most of the trees in Central Park are deciduous, and they are busy leafing out. Not so much, though, that I can't see around me. I can tell that the farther north I go in the park the more the walkers are native New Yorkers, not tourists. How do I know that? They don't have shopping bags. They don't cling to their partners like lovers. They have an attitude like this is *their* park, and this is something they do everyday. I wish we had a park like this in Sun Prairie where people could feel like they owned it.

It's almost mid-day, and the park is overrun with people and dogs. When I arrive at the Reservoir, I recognize it. A walking/running path surrounds the round body of water that once supplied New York City with its water. I read this on a plaque. A three-pronged fountain spits forth near the original water power plant. The whole surface is contained by a chain-link fence to keep out swimmers and boaters I assume. Outer paths surround the Reservoir, some meant for walkers, some for horses. I couldn't care less as I walk aimlessly around this mesmerizing body of water searching for my nemesis.

Here's how Mom told it: "I went into the park everyday before you were born, and one day I saw something I'd never seen before. It was different from everything around it. It was majestic, a deep green. It was evergreen. Garlands of tufted pine needles fell from its branches. Then one day I came to visit my newest best friend, and snow had settled on each pine needle. I shivered and suddenly, so did the tree. A shower of white fell to the ground. I shivered again and so did the tree. There were only two trees like this in the whole park. Most had leaves that dropped in fall. This tree was unique. It had a plaque and was the largest of the two. The plaque read: Atlas Cedar. I would name my son after this tree."

I find that tree, the plaque, the whole bit and feel no remorse at shooting a dart at the heart of its trunk.

I still haven't told my shirt-tail relatives why I came, but finally I had to say my name. I'm AC to friends, but that gets into that whole AC/DC thing, so I call myself Ace to strangers. That causes plenty of problems, too. Those relatives in New Jersey asked what my sport was.

Archery, I said.

HOUSE OF MIRRORS

Though the world goes on about me, I swear I pick and choose my way. Except now I'm not so sure, especially when I look in the mirror and see my white-haired mother. I've always hated white hair, especially on women. Besides, I'd always thought I looked like my father.

While my mother was alive, I chose to be involved in those aspects of her life that I could relate to, those parts that would please us both. Everything else I did was appropriately altruistic, the inner city work, the Brain Research Foundation, but she didn't seem to understand. Why don't you join a Garden Club, she would ask viewing a publicity picture of me receiving some important trophy from an inner city youth group. I never had trouble taking a stand. It all seemed obvious to me, and I'd vehemently try to explain.

But lately I've been plagued by hindsight. My visionary stands have become fuzzy. I visited Mom and Dad often throughout their life span; it was easier after I became their parent. That happened early on. I had no problem with it, I was the problem solver. I was around. I thought I had the solutions and was supplying them with the answers they needed. It never occurred to me that my mother had answers too, answers I rejected early on along with her white hair.

While she was sick and close to dying, I felt a certain resentment. Perhaps because we were very different people, and she never accepted that as easily as I did. I think she wanted a clone.

In their late seventies Mom and Dad moved to an adult retirement community in Florida. They should have moved there long before they did because Mom had been sick for a long time, not bed-ridden, though, and this turned out to be her kind of place. People there were into luncheons and bridge groups. Boring for me, but I saw how important it was for Mom.

Now I wonder just what did I expect from my parents in their old age? I'm not sure, but I know what I didn't expect — to inherit their old-age image. As I've said, I always hated white hair. I never knew my mother without white hair. I hated it to the point that in middle-aged desperation I started coloring my own hair the minute a trace of white appeared. A victim of advertising I'm ashamed to admit, I've finally stopped coloring my hair. It took a lot of courage. So now do I pride myself on not being phony? — what you see is what you get? Or did I let it go 'natural' simply because dyed white hair turns blond then purple, and that looks really disgusting. Do I like me less now that I have finally succumbed to letting my hair go white? Where's my self-esteem when I look in the mirror and see my mother's white hair that was always so 'not for me.' The man who cuts my hair says, "I see possibilities." I don't trust him.

I look at people who say "I love your hair" squarely in the face. They have dyed hair, for heaven's sake, and I don't know what to say. Of course, now I wonder why they keep coloring their hair. I want to ask, "Why do you still color your hair if you think mine looks so great?" Is it because they're simply so used to it or is it because their husbands don't like women with white hair? Maybe a white-haired lady reminds the husband of his aging (never mind that he hasn't bothered to color his own disappearing grey strands). Could these women possibly think I can't tell? Perhaps they simply cannot defy their hairdresser who says, "I could enhance this."

Lately I've been asking my friends if they want to be like their mother. The responses are three-to-one a vehement "no." I'm not sure I like my survey results. At first I was gratified because it supported my theory — eased the guilt I feel about not wanting to be like my mother. On the other hand, it confuses the issue. It's disheartening to think my children might side with the majority. Perhaps I'm putting too much blame on the fact my mother stood for some things I cannot bear to find in myself. What is it they say… "Those who don't know their history are destined to repeat it." But what if one can't fathom that until it's too late.

My niece recently spent two years searching for her birth mother whom she found. The ramifications of this intrigue me. At first Sarah was fascinated to discover common physical characteristics with her birth mother. I wonder what Sarah would answer if I asked if she wants to be like her birth mother. Could it be one of the subliminal reasons for her search?

I doubt if my own mother ever faced these questions because her mother died when she was nine, and she had to assume a parental role for younger siblings at a very young age. I'm respecting that now, but that's not helped solve the dilemma of why I hate white hair.

Unfortunately, I live in a house with a ton of mirrors. It does my ego no good to pass them continually and see no one other than my mother whose white hair I'd early on programmed myself to detest. I remind myself of coming to visit her one time and thinking as I rode the escalator down to the baggage claim how good-looking she was as she awaited my arrival.

I arrived in Florida a couple of hours after she had died. The funeral directors were at the house, and the hearse was still parked in the carport. I discovered she had already been removed from her bed, bagged and was about to be transported to the funeral home. It didn't take me long to know I must ask to see her. I was very sad not to have been there when she died because I had come so many times on the spur of the moment when Dad thought she was dying. I felt cheated not to be there, and now I wanted to experience the finality of it. They opened the back of the hearse and pulled out the stretcher holding the zippered bag that housed my mother. I asked them to open it. I didn't know what I expected to see, but I had to see for myself that she had died, not just be told. I'd only known her alive. Death is so scary. She was cold, I know because I touched her. Her mouth was open and without teeth because she'd worn false teeth for many years, but I was used to seeing her toothless. Her head was thrust back a bit. I cried. I cried because she had wanted so desperately to live, and I cried because suddenly she stood for a lot more than her dreaded legacy of white hair. My first thought was how nice she would no longer suffer from the liver disease that had plagued her the last twenty-five years — not yet realizing how much I would miss her.

On the other hand, my mother had some martyr blood

in her, and she'd handled her illness quite well. I often thought she was more comfortable in illness than in health. I never noticed her white hair as I stood there. It didn't matter — I was still coloring my own tresses their 'original' color.

I get teary when I find a recipe that I treasure written in her own hand. What bothers me the most, though, is my continual missing her. I think of her more than when she was alive. It kills me to think my children would think of me so seldom until after I was dead.

Then I pass another damned mirror and see that reflection. The parental guillotine descends upon my arrogance with a clean swift swipe, and here I stand — white hair in hand.

I can't bring myself to say 'my' white hair. It's still hers. And I haven't joined a Garden Club either — but I'm considering it.

LAST NIGHT'S HERO

"What a night!" Carol closed the ornate iron gate and looked around the quaint courtyard. "This is — something else."

George pressed the doorbell at the pink stone villa. "Barnes must be doing all right."

Purple and white flowers tumbled from vines that clung tight to the wall. Carol sniffed the air. "Just like I remember — flowers, romance."

"What the hell?" George pushed the bell a second time and looked at his watch. "Seven o'clock. Don't suppose we're late, do you?"

"I don't think so. Everything is late in Italy."

"Remember, Carol, Barnes is an American."

Suddenly the large wooden door opened, and Peter Barnes stood before them, arms extended. Guiding them into the marble-floored foyer, he kissed Carol on the cheek, then guffawed his "old-buddy" laugh pumping George's arm up and down.

"So good to see you. Sorry to keep you waiting. Antonio was just finishing a story. Come on, we're out on the *terrazza*. How's my Italian?" He winked at Carol. "It's about time you and Antonio meet, George. You've only been doing business together for — let's see — three years now?"

"Thanks to you," George said.

"Here we are! Antonio, meet the President and founder of Winters Scientific, Mr. George Winters and his beautiful wife, Carol. Well," Peter said clapping his hands together, "opposite sides of the ocean meet at last. What do we call it? Free trade, open market, whatever! Hah, hah," he laughed and gave George a couple of hearty thumps on the back.

Carol stepped onto the terrace, all smiles feeling as though she were on stage. "Antonio." She extended her hand, intrigued with the idea of an Italian man, at once admiring his piercing brown eyes.

Antonio bowed and took her hand. "Buona sera, signora."

"Buona sera," she answered.

"So, you speak Italian."

"Not really." She blushed. She noticed a slight balding at Antonio's hair line, but decided it added to his good looks. Even the slight paunch above his belt did not detract from his charm.

"George," Peter interjected, "come sit here, next to Antonio. I'll go mix some drinks. Carol, would you like to see the villa?"

"Indeed," and reluctantly followed him into the house.

Carol returned to the terrace as quickly as possible. The men were busily talking and sipping their drinks. Carol overheard her name and paused to listen. George was holding forth.

"You know, Antonio, you and I might have met long before but for some glamorous Italian count Carol keeps bringing up. He was *some* guy, according to her. She won't let me forget it." George smiled proudly, "She was almost a countess, you know."

"Now George," Carol interrupted, aware of Antonio's eyes following her across the terrace. "Let me tell it, George. You make it sound so frivolous."

"I want to hear *this*." Peter pulled up a chair. "But first some wine. No stories on an empty stomach."

"Mille grazie," Carol said, looking at Antonio for his approval.

Antonio raised his glass. "Salute!"

She smiled back, fingering her entwined Cartier bracelets. "Well," Carol began, "I know you've heard this before, George, but be patient — and don't interrupt." Everyone laughed. "You see, Antonio, the big thing to do — twenty years ago, that is," she laughed, "after your sophomore year in college, *and* your second year of Italian, was to spend six weeks in Italy. Well," she continued, "three of us came to Rome one summer, stayed at the Esperia on Firenza — near the Borghese Palace. I remember that anyway."

Antonio nodded in agreement. "All girls?"

Feeling the wine, she nodded, "I just loved it, took some classes in Italian, toured the sights, did it all. But the last week we were here," she paused dramatically. "I fell *in love*," she drawled. "I did — at first sight. I'll never forget it. We met these boys, I mean, young Italian men," correcting herself before George could. "They were sooo mature. We met them at an elegant outdoor cafe, a trattoria. For the life of me, I can't remember which one, but it was close to the Piazza del Bernini. One of the young men was especially handsome. Well, that was it! We saw each other every minute. He took me everywhere, even if I'd already seen it." She continued fervently, "The last day I found out he was royalty. Would you believe?"

She stopped abruptly when Maria announced the antipasto di mare was served. Peter led them around the corner of the terrace to a round glass-top table, complete with flickering candles.

"*Very* nice, Peter," Carol said.

Antonio touched her forearm, and she motioned him to sit next to her.

"Go on, what happened next, Carol?"

"Oh, nothing, really. I couldn't give him my address because I knew my parents would kill me." She sighed. "He would remain a perfect memory. Oh my, my Italian count!"

The table fell silent. Carol luxuriated in the moment. Maria moved about them clearing the first course and refilling wine glasses.

Antonio lifted his glass of wine and gazed at it, "Superbo."

Carol watched the sun filtering through his wine. Evening light was approaching an artistic height, gilding wherever it touched.

Antonio lifted his glass high. "Only good wine glows in the light of an Italian evening," Antonio mused, "and beautiful women." Toasting Carol seemed to trigger some special memory. He smiled as though remembering something unforgettable and took a long slow sip from his now consecrated wine.

"Ahhh!" he sighed with satisfaction, "those American women!"

They looked at Antonio.

No one spoke, least of all Antonio. Maria appeared with the main course. "Grazie, Maria," Peter complimented her.

"Superbo," Antonio added exuberantly. "My favorite — Scalloppina de Vitello."

Maria smiled and quickly filled his glass with vino rosso.

Antonio settled back in his chair. "I, too, remember summers, Carol, and, believe it or not, I remember the American women. So beautiful! I would go with my friends looking for them, the young American women who came for the summer. They were *so* lovely, *so* fair. Ah, yes, to further their education — at the trattorias."

Everyone laughed.

He turned to Carol. "As you said, Carol, and usually at the Capriccio, in late afternoons, groups of three or four. The Capriccio was, as you say in the U.S., a hangout."

"The Capriccio?" Carol said softly. "I think I remember that."

"What was your friend's name?" Antonio asked. "Perhaps I knew him."

"You know, it's funny, but I can't even remember his name anymore."

"We never said our real names," Antonio confessed. "We lied. Wasn't that awful? We were very bad."

"Oh, I don't know," George interjected. "Sounds like some of the things we used to do. I'll never forget the time..."

Carol shook her head at George, sighing with relief when Peter interrupted to ask Maria about the dessert. "Something elegant, I'm sure."

"Limone sorbetto," Maria proudly announced.

"Perfetto," Peter nodded.

Carol leaned close to Antonio. "What name did you use, Antonio, with those American girls. Who were you?"

"Nino, I was Nino."

Excusing herself from the table, she stumbled over her chair leg. Numbly, she walked across the harsh-sounding marble floor, searching for the bathroom. Once inside, she leaned against the door, her heart pounding fiercely. She groped for the light and was shocked to see her reflection in the mirror. She looked old, lined, greying, everything she dreaded. Oh, God! I've got to get out of here before he remembers me. Even so, she took a minute to put on fresh eye shadow and dab her wrinkles with powder. She smoothed her hair and hurried back to the table.

Approaching George from behind, she whispered they must leave, soon. "Don't ask why," she warned.

Awkwardly, she sat down and grabbed her spoon without a glance toward Antonio.

They finished dessert and caffè in awkward silence. George stood and dutifully offered their apologies for leaving so early — "tomorrow's meetings," nodding to Antonio.

Antonio rose, politely excusing himself.

Carol scurried toward the door when Antonio touched her arm and spun her around to face him. He leaned very close.

His cheek all but touched hers. "The Capriccio — tomorrow — noon?" Not waiting for an answer, he brushed her cheek with his lips. "Ciao!"

Silently, George and Carol drove back to the Villa Belvedere. A soft breeze blew Carol's hair across her face as she nestled against the car seat.

George stopped for a red light and looked over at her. "What did Antonio say when he pulled you aside?"

Carol stared out the open window.

George shook her gently. "Well?"

"Ciao," she whispered. "He said 'Ciao.'"
"I thought that meant Hello."
"It means Goodbye, Hello, See you later — "
"Oh," George shrugged as the light turned green.

STRIKE UP THE BAND

I haven't figured out being sixty yet. During that decade Dad lost his job, found a new one, had to move and managed two heart attacks. Now he wants me to understand being ninety.

The occasion is Dad's ninetieth birthday. I've struggled with it for some time. Should I organize a gala celebration or do the usual—send a card, rack my brain for a present or just call? Besides where would the celebration be? I live in Detroit, and he lives in Florida. I haven't much enthusiasm for what it would take to pull together a ninetieth birthday party in an adult community in Florida, keep it a surprise, figure out whom to invite, food, flowers — ugh.

My friend Tom's tale keeps recycling through my mind. He'd gone to a ton of work and expense gathering the family and his father's one old friend to create a one-hundredth birthday party for his dad. The truth was old C.T. would rather have served in Desert Storm than be center stage at his one-hundredth birthday. Tom even took the trouble to have Willard Scott announce C.T.'s birthday on the Today show. Sharp as he was, C.T. never caught it because Willard mispronounced his name so badly.

With that scenario in mind, I scuttle a party in Florida. It isn't until Dad's lady friend in Florida says to me, "I wouldn't have expected you to think of it," that a birthday plan pops defensively into my head.

I tell Dad we are going to a family picnic. Each year the Sanders family reunion had lured him back to the area where he was born and spent his childhood. For several years he's been the oldest living relative and loves it, so that hurdle isn't hard.

To my surprise the affair turns out quite simple to juggle by phone. White Pines State Park, where our family had often picnicked, has a rustic restaurant that will arrange a buffet complete with birthday cake. I call some of his relatives, rely on word of mouth, and the birthday is billed as an Open House in three small local newspapers. MAN IS 90 one local paper reports.

The day before his birthday Dad and I meet in Chicago and drive to the heart of the cornbelt, Rochelle, Illinois, the closest town that could support a motel. He made the room reservation, just one of course, for the sake of economy, he says. I have white hair and everything that goes with it, and Dad looks especially young. I turn away to avoid the receptionist's controlled smile.

The morning of the Celebration Dad wants to tour the familiar thirty square mile area where he grew up. We start early and stop a thousand times while he describes a relative or friend who'd lived here or there and what they'd done. Four brothers, of which Dad is the oldest, were born within five years, and he remembers being farmed out — often.

Soon I can imagine the people he describes, feel their ancient bearded stubble, sense their pulsing frontier energy.

An impenetrable silence cloaks one homestead to the next. Time slips backward. Now I even hear their voices though no one is home where we stop and stare. Through Dad's nostalgic wanderings, folks hoe in the back field, harness the horse and buggy for a trip to town — milk lowing cows in the barn.

By mid-morning our imaginations are so well honed that we find plump Aunt Lucy at home in her old-fashioned Victorian farmhouse, grey hair braided in a crown about her head. She opens the back door to greet us (front doors were never used and remained forebodingly locked). Wiping wet hands on a spanking clean apron, she smiles, wide-eyed and gap-toothed. She mouths words we can only imagine. We know she's glad to see us, but not nearly as happy as we are to rediscover her. She motions by a sweep of her hand, and we look toward the barn where Uncle Chet pitches straw into a mud-soaked cow lot. He props an elbow on his pitchfork when he sees her. Every few words he lets out another swear word that isn't at all offensive because we can't hear him. We laugh. We love everyone we see this morning. How little we leave behind save our silent voices.

We still have enough time to stop at the Ashton cemetery where we find everyone at home. My mother is also buried in this cemetery. We stand in front of her grave and once again read the names on her gravestone. It is Dad's marker, too. He'd blocked in his own name alongside hers to save money.

"Looks real nice, doesn't it?" he proudly announces more than asks.

His name, Frederick Theodore Sanders, is below hers on the same stone. His birth date is engraved below his name: August 30, 1902, but of course there is a blank space after Died. He'd wanted to engrave the numbers of the 20th century, leaving the year open, but everyone thought he looked too healthy.

Less than a year ago my brother died. He had asked to be buried in the plot next to Dad and Mom. Ted's grave is directly to the right. An American Legion plaque has fallen across the stone marker. Dad picks it up and tries to force it into the ground behind the marker, but the earth proves too hard to penetrate. He puts it back down as he found it and speaks lovingly of Ted's graveside service. His memories are different from mine.

Apparently, the new minister in town had mistakenly researched Dad's history, not Ted's (his nickname), all because their names were the same. Dad, in fact, heard his own eulogy that day. He never acknowledged it, but I'd have told him it's not all bad to appear live and listen to your own eulogy.

I think of all this while Dad and I look at our relatives' graves. I am relieved that the MAN IS 90 article in the local paper is celebrating a man's birthday and not his death.

After lunch we decide to take a short nap before the birthday party. The maid has not made up the room yet and not wanting to be wakened in the middle of our rest, Dad hangs out the DO NOT DISTURB sign at noon. We sleep undisturbed. Before leaving the motel we see the maid down the hall, and he calls to her. "You're free to make up our room now." I don't wait to catch her expression.

I am very nervous before arriving at what I hope is to be the ultimate glorification of Dad's life, although it will be hard to top the eulogy. What if no one comes?

The private room at the restaurant is pine-paneled, just the right size, plenty of tables, and the buffet looks sumptuous. Across from the buffet is a table where there are two sheet cakes frosted white with "Happy Birthday, Fred" and written below is "From your Families" in yellow frosting. I can't remember requesting "From your Families," but it looks good anyway.

Coming in I'd spotted a perky bouquet of black-eyed Susans in the lobby, and now I retreat to borrow them for a couple of hours. They complement the yellow lettering on the cake. Dad is not at all surprised at the preparations and, in fact, seems quite pleased.

About then the photographer I'd hired arrives. We must record such an event — that is, if it turns into an event.

One cousin and her husband arrive shortly before the appointed hour and are too shy to submit to a formal portrait with Dad. They won't be much consolation, either, in case they turn out to be the only guests. The food-laden buffet is reminiscent of one of those bountiful farm feasts after haymaking, but looks ludicrous with only the four of us to eat. The cousins keep Dad busy talking.

Then my husband and two daughters arrive along with my niece's family. I begin to relax as a few others drift into the room. These people still have rural roots, farm folk to the core, and they haven't a clue of how to barge in. Instead they amble in, somewhat shyly, making sure they're in the right place. They come in family groups of two and three generations, wander to an empty table and position themselves around it, patiently waiting for Dad to come over and greet them.

Dad is in high form. He looks and acts eons younger than his ninety years. He makes the rounds, sporting a smile he couldn't have erased if he tried. Tables and chairs fill, and the room begins to hum as one remembrance builds upon another. Only the best is recalled — those delectable nubbins left clinging to the edges of memories, time having consumed the distasteful portions.

"Uncle Fred," says Dad's Uncle Chet's grandchild, a woman already in her fifties, "tell us again about when you pushed Mom in Kyte Creek and she almost..., right, Mom?" She nudges her mother who smirks in retaliation.

"Hey, Fred, ask if she's got any witnesses?" a younger cousin, Lord knows how many generations removed, calls out.

Dad laughs. "You get this old, witnesses are a thing of the past. I can't even carry a grudge anymore — can't remember what made me mad."

On and on trail the memories, detailed by one generation to the next.

The highlight is when a former girlfriend of Dad's arrives with her sister and a friend. I can tell he still likes her because he ushers her to a table in the center of the room and asks the photographer to take several pictures of them together.

The celebration is a definite success. At least fifty people come. I've lost count. A curtain drawn across one end of the room conceals a stage. As people rise to leave Dad pulls the curtain aside and announces, "See this stage? Ten years from now we'll all come back — and — we'll hire a band!"

When everyone finally eases their way out, and the last hand is squeezed, my daughter, Dana, asks if we can go to see Grandma's grave.

The sun has set by the time we pull into the little Ashton cemetery. A darkening sky burns red where a fat sun has just vacated. Gravestones and stately pines are silhouetted against the evening's infancy, as is my daughter. She moves like a dancer midst the stoic markers, heralding their stature. For the first time I notice she is carrying a small bunch of flowers, the black-eyed Susans she doesn't know I'd pilfered to enhance the birthday cake. Her moves are exaggerated in contrast to the stationary stones. Dad and I watch her lithe form bend forward, as in prayer. She places the bouquet on my mother's, Dad's wife's, her grandmother's grave.

She rises, looks down at her offering and says, "I wanted to include Grandma in the party."

ON BEING ALONE

I can't believe it's almost over — ten days alone. I've built a lot of fires. I'm watching the four-foot fire poker move against the fireplace back and forth, hanging from its hook. I know from experience with an ancient petulant clock exactly when a pendulum decides to be self-motivating, and this one's not going to make it. Too bad, it's trying so hard, but I suppose it would be an extraordinary fluke if a common fire poker could sustain perpetual motion.

This has to do with imagination.

I take long, long walks. On one walk I was so moved by the light, the air, the silence, the importance of the moment that I struggled to record it so it would never be lost. One thing is for sure — it would not be the same if someone were here with me.

Each day I search for the ultimate walk. I've found it, I say. The lane leading into the logger's road is canopied by yellow, orange and green. I lose control. I can but follow. I pull the car to one side and start out, drawn to where I've never been, where I've never walked. The logger's path continues on, but I see another off-shoot of what may have been another logger's road from long ago and follow it. The sun slithers through tall, old maples. I've never been in this room. It's a world-sized fairyland stage scaled down just for me. I could scream and no one would hear. I could weep and no one would hug me. I am here, once exposed never to lose the image and hear the music of intimacy.

I walk indefinitely. I've turned inside out and stride with the innermost part on the outside. How weird to expose that section where the passionate core of the heart and the rational mind come together, where the soul sneaks around, craving to feel beyond. It's in slow motion, parading a trinity that I pray will never end. I find where I'm going although I've not ended my walk and hope I never will.

I accept the fact that I am addicted to atmospheres created by me, I must confess, but influenced by environs that inspire. It buys me a good seat in the arena of imagination.

The family will arrive tomorrow. What have I done that I can tell them? The walks. The writing. Swinging fire pokers. The nagging loneliness. Give me a break their eyes will say.

But I know what's happened, and it has to do with me and my imagination.

A few years ago I went to England alone to walk and to write and discover about being alone. I'd read an article in *The New York Times Book Review* about Thomas Wolfe who'd gone to London to walk and to write. So one April, I decided to follow his romantic-sounding regime: rise early, walk in the West Sussex countryside, return to an English breakfast, write in the Inn's library for a few hours, snack for lunch, tour neighboring sights in my car, nap a bit, bathe, then wine and dinner while writing in my journal. My family was appalled when I broke the news. A middle-aged woman alone? To walk and to write? Jubilant while planning the trip, I almost bailed out over the Atlantic flying to where not one soul would recognize me. Not that I was so recognizable anywhere, but I worried about getting so homesick that I couldn't stay afloat. I can still see my husband shaking his head in disbelief.

Somehow I found the small village of Thakeham in West Sussex, a twelfth-century hamlet two hours south of London that wants to remain just that, ancient and hidden. I'd booked my stay at Abingworth Hall surrounded by rolling countryside as advertised. Shadowing Thomas Wolfe's wanderlust, I knew I would fall prey to England's labyrinth of footpaths, lose myself to the ancient Saxons and write a bestseller.

My knees buckled the minute I entered Abingworth Hall. The proprietor was indeed courteous, but I could sense he thought me mad. The room was smaller than I'd imagined but did have a quaint dormer.

I rose promptly at 7 a.m., donned my boots, raincoat and earmuffs, and ignoring all side glances stepped into a cold hazy April morning in Britain. Within minutes I stumbled upon a footpath sign not more than a stone's throw from a busy modern thoroughfare. By the time I reached the next footpath sign, I was hooked. Not only had I passed authentic, lived in, sixteenth-century thatched cottages, I was walking an ancient map alive with acres of daffodils beyond belief.

"Follow your nose," the British say. Beckoned by the sea breeze, I tromped through history. The road ended, but I succumbed to the weathered moss-green footpath arrow, climbed a stile, crossed a meadow and found myself on a ridge overlooking a luxuriant valley that swept up to the South Downs, an elevated chalk spine that serpentines its way through Southern England near the sea. I recognized the awesome Chactonbury Ring atop the Downs, a stand of trees that dates back to the Iron Age.

I passed through what had been William Penn's fields before he opted to settle his family and the Quakers in Pennsylvania. How could he leave such a Paradise? What became a daily route led me through a woodland glade of bluebells, winding through ancient Thakeham with its own twelfth-century church, pub and post office. What I wasn't prepared for was the nagging loneliness, but that's what made me write.

It was the Post Mistress who introduced me to the community. Each morning as I finished my walk, I stopped by with another letter to mail. I tried not to be too nosy, but I discovered the British are not aloof, just shy. The Post Mistress introduced me to the Vicar's wife, the pub owner, a local socialite and the President of the local Women's Club. That's about all I could handle after the invitations to tea, sherry, club meetings and dinners. So much for the nagging loneliness that fed my need to write.

I never did get to meet the "brothers" who lived along the ancient flowering sunken path that wound through the small village of Thakeham. It was two days before it was discovered one had died and only then because he hadn't touched his afternoon tea.

My husband arrived the last few days of my stay. They told him no one had ever stayed so long with them.

The trip became my pilgrimage. I learned that once my imagination is whetted, there is no end to the journey. Unfortunately, to develop this I need to be alone. There should be some formula to find the perfect balance between loneliness and being alone.

Now in my seventies, by the time I have spare moments, I'm so brainwashed by the twenty-minute fragment syndrome (just how long *did* it take me to make the bed, pick up the kids, find the blown fuse, snowblow the driveway) that guilt still consumes me if I spend an hour with myself. So I keep busy — join a club, play golf, volunteer, exercise, whatever.

I must practice being alone. The future can only be imagined. It's my glimpse of Hope, my take on what's to come.

So I walk to be possessed by nightly calm and smells of morning.

What critics say about

June: A Novel
By Mary Sanders Smith

With warmly assembled details, Smith neatly captures the ways and the politics of a pre-WWII farm community, and the segments concerning Frank Lloyd Wright are also well researched.... Smith... pull[s] off a detailed story about a woman, a time, and a way of life often overlooked.
Publishers Weekly

Not since John Steinbeck has the modern novel been able to present a rural voice as rich as that of Mary Sanders Smith. To discover her is to begin a life-long love affair with the literature of our time.
Loren D. Estleman, novelist

A rare contemporary novel that shows American farm life just before WWII. New energy and greater abundance – caused in part by Roosevelt's Secretary of Agriculture, Henry Wallace – are mirrored by new-found desires and opportunities in the farmer's wife, June. Her awakening is sparked by Frank Lloyd Wright's work and by a new hired hand. A great read. It's so visual it will make a great movie.
Edith Chevat, novelist and associate editor of *Global Review*

| ***June: A Novel*** | $16 Paperback | 0-931642-29-9 |
| | $26 Hardcover | 0-931642-30-2 |

**To order *June* or *Love Takes*
Call 1-866-390-9666
or Fax 1-715-424-0909**